Arc Over Time

Jen Silver

Arc Over Time

Sequel to Starting Over

Jen Silver

An Affinity Romance

Affinity
eBook Press
NZ
2015

Arc Over Time

© Jen Silver 2015

Affinity E-Book Press NZ LTD
Canterbury, New Zealand

1st Edition

ISBN: 978-1-927328-78-1

All rights reserved.

Editor: Ruth Stanley
Proof Editor: Alexis Smith
Cover Design: Irish Dragon Designs

Acknowledgments

Thanks go to the wonderful team at Affinity eBook Press for their continuing encouragement and professionalism. Thank you to my beta readers who said they were happy to read more about the characters from *Starting Over*. Some ace beta editing by Kay and Mel helped to hone the manuscript so that Ruth's task on the final editing stage was, hopefully, less arduous.

But my most heartfelt thanks go to Nancy K who surely demonstrated the patience of a saint when faced with the job of creating just the right cover for this book. And I feel she's succeeded magnificently.

Thank you also to all the readers and reviewers of my debut novel *Starting Over*. I hope you will enjoy this one, as it is a continuation of the characters' journeys, digging a little deeper into their lives.

This book is dedicated to my mother who has always been my inspiration to keep writing.

And, as ever, I acknowledge the love and strength given to me on a daily basis by my loving partner of nearly thirty years, Anne.

Dedication

For Rachel

Table of Contents

Also By Jen Silver

There Was a Time
Starting Over
Affinity's 2014 Christmas Collection

Part One

Chapter One

Meetings

"She calls, you go running." Jasmine looked at her friend in disgust. "Aren't you fed up being second best?"

Denise glanced out the café window. Jas always insisted they go to Starbucks even though she knew her friend wasn't keen on supporting the franchise. "They stood up for gay marriage," she would say to appease her. Den would have preferred her usual haunt, the French bakery on the Marylebone High Street.

It was true she hadn't hesitated in agreeing to meet the professor off the train when she'd phoned the night before. It had been a month now since they'd gone to the wedding at Starling Hill and the night of passion Den had hoped for on that occasion hadn't materialised. Instead, the night was spent consoling the older woman. Watching the 'love of her life' marry a woman she despised had proved more than Kathryn could handle.

Poking around the remnants of the cappuccino froth in her mug, Den finally looked up. "We're friends, that's all. She knows she can talk to me."

"Well, she needs to change the record. It's getting boring. And I know you want more from the relationship than holding hands."

Den sighed. She couldn't argue with that. Jas had a way of getting straight to the point. They'd known each other since high school. She recalled that first day, a nightmare, trying to find her way around a building the size of a prison and twice as intimidating. Jas had been lost as well and they met in a dark downstairs hallway leading nowhere. It was an unlikely pairing. In their first year, Jas soon got in with the popular girls, discussing boys and makeup with ease. Den was always an outsider. She hung around with the other misfits, getting kicked out of classes, smoking in the toilets, frequenting the after-school club known as Detention.

Things changed in their second year. Jasmine had tired of the empty-headed views of her peers and persuaded Den to join her in the library at lunchtimes. They read books, shared ideas, and became politically aware. With encouragement from their English teacher, they started a newspaper. Suddenly, they were the cool ones. Kids who had ignored them before now wanted to be in their gang.

It was no surprise they both chose careers that involved writing. Jasmine Pepper was in public relations, mistress of the beguiling press release, and Denise Sullivan was a reporter. Her journalistic career had mostly been low-level, covering minor local events, until the year before when Jas introduced her to Dr Kathryn Moss, a professor of archaeology at a northern university. Reporting on the extraordinary finds at Starling Hill and using some underhanded methods, she had finally made it, her byline on the front page of a national newspaper. The fame had come at a cost, and her hopes of a more permanent relationship with Dr Moss had derailed before it really started. There was a mutual attraction though, and when they met up, more often than not, they would have sex.

As if reading her mind, Jasmine broke into her thoughts, saying, "Come on, Den. All you get from her is a comfort fuck now and then."

"Yeah, well, something's better than nothing." She would be seeing Kathryn again in an hour's time and it was all she could do to keep her body still.

"I don't know why she's hung up on Eleanor what's-her-face, anyway. Stuck-up, bitch."

"Now who's got a hang-up? I thought you were over Robin."

"Robin who?"

Jasmine's studied indifference didn't fool Den. Jasmine had been in love with Robin Fanshawe and thought their affair meant something. Jas still couldn't believe that Robin had gone through with marrying Ellie. And, it seemed, Kathryn hadn't got over that either. Den stood up, unable to stay seated any longer.

"Gotta go, Jas. Don't want to keep the lady waiting."

"You never do. Good luck, anyway."

†

Den huddled into her jacket, the cold easterly wind dramatically lowering the temperature of what had earlier seemed like a nice June day. Making her way to King's Cross train station to meet Kathryn, she wondered what mood she would be in. Their phone conversation the night before had been brief. Kathryn hadn't even said why she was coming to London.

She really hoped they weren't going to be rehashing the wedding. It had been upsetting to see Kathryn's pain. The professor had thought going to the wedding would help her get over Ellie's rejection. Instead it had just intensified her distress at what she had lost. Den thought Kathryn was probably deluding herself about what their affair had meant to

Ellie. From what she had seen when she met them, Ellie was devoted to Robin.

Checking the arrivals board it looked like the Leeds train was on time. Den waited by the platform exit point. She checked her phone again. No messages. Not even an 'I'm on the train' one. So, it looked like Kathryn was in a non-communicative mood. Hopefully lunch at their favourite restaurant in Soho would jolt Kathryn out of whatever hurt she was carrying around.

People started coming through the gate. With her height, Den could see over most heads. The first-class carriage would be at the front of the train so she shouldn't have long to wait.

✝

Kathryn saw Den as she passed through the ticket barrier. There was no mistaking her tall form, shaggy hair standing on end, looking as if she'd just got out of bed. Whose bed, she wondered? But she didn't really have any right to ask.

"Hey, Prof. Over here!"

Kathryn smiled. It was hard not to when greeted by Den's enthusiasm. She let the taller woman pull her into a hug.

"Thanks for meeting me," she said when Den released her.

"Can't have you wandering around the big city on your own." Den took her briefcase from her. "Is this all you've got?"

"Yes. I'm only here for one night. Change of underwear and toothbrush."

"So, what's the occasion?"

"Second interview at UCL." Den's look of delight didn't escape her notice. "Don't get too excited. At the moment it's a toss up between here and Durham."

"Durham! You can't be serious."

"Why not? They're up there with Oxford and Cambridge as far as archaeology's concerned."

"It's only about a thousand miles from here!"

Kathryn laughed. "Two hundred and seventy-five, actually."

"Far enough."

It wasn't difficult to read Den. Kathryn knew she wanted more from her. She had tried very hard to let go of her feelings for Eleanor Winters. But it proved difficult. Everything she did now tied in to the events of the previous year at Starling Hill farm, Ellie's home. Every time she spoke at a convention the topic everyone wanted her to discuss was the discovery of Queen Cartimandua's burial place. Happy to use the boost to her credentials that the excavation of the bones had given her and with that the chance to make a move to a more prestigious university, there were some memories of the dig that she knew should be left behind. In particular, the memory of a night of passion with Ellie when she had dared to hope that it would lead to something more—maybe the long-term relationship that had always eluded her. Ellie had shattered that dream and married Robin. It was time she moved on.

"What time's your interview?"

Den's question pulled her back into the present.

"Four thirty."

"Good, plenty of time for a psychological adjustment, then." Den had expertly maneuvered them into a taxi.

"I can't turn up reeking of drink."

"A glass of wine with lunch isn't likely to harm your chances. And I'd say you need a drink to help you loosen up a bit."

Over lunch they stuck to general topics. By the time they'd finished their main courses the weather and politics had been thoroughly covered. Den had recovered her cool demeanour but Kathryn wasn't taken in. It was all or nothing with Den. And she knew the journalist wanted it to be all. She still wasn't sure she wanted to live in London if they offered her the job. The idea of being at the centre of things was appealing, close to the museums and galleries. But every time she returned to her northern home, she felt the draw of the open spaces, the hills and deep valleys; the mysteries still to be unearthed. If only it didn't also remind her of a certain blonde with beguiling blue eyes. London would offer many distractions, and one of them was sitting in front of her. She met Den's questioning gaze and smiled.

"I'll text you when I'm finished."

"How long will it take?"

"I've no idea. There will be more in-depth questions about my area of research. And I will have to negotiate on the number of teaching hours they expect from me."

†

After her coffee with Den, Jasmine walked back to her office deep in thought. Watching Den enjoy her frothy cappuccino while she sipped at her Americano, sans sugar, sans milk, sans taste had been a form of torture. Her friend could eat and drink what she liked and stay rail thin. Jas had to count every calorie to keep her weight down. Den had also never seen the inside of a gym. But Den at least had the glimmer of a sex life, even if it was with the elusive professor. Jas was finding it hard to be interested in the scene, to even think about dating again. The emotional fallout from

Robin's defection had hit her harder than she'd thought at the time. It was almost a year now since that ill-fated trip to Starling Hill. She had been in love. Or was it just in lust? Robin had never given her anything other than the most amazing sexual experiences.

Time to get her mind back on work. Her assistant, Ray, met her at the door.

"Thank God. I was going to send out a search party."

Jasmine eyed him suspiciously. "Why, what's up?"

"That new client. They want to see us an hour earlier."

"Shit! Have you got the proposal?"

"Yup. Two copies, printed and bound."

"Great." She turned on her heel. "Taxi ordered?"

"Should be here now."

A black cab was just turning the corner as they walked out onto the street. Settling back in the seat, Jas took a copy of the proposal from Ray and flicked through it. Their research had been pretty thorough but she didn't want to be hit with any surprises. This was a big project and they would only get one chance to pitch for the business. They were meeting the marketing director, Max Fleetwood. *Wonder if he got teased at school, Fleetwood Max, ha-ha. Better give that a miss.*

†

The company's headquarters, all chrome and glass, complete with upper-class receptionist, looked suitably impressive. They were directed to the uncomfortable-looking seats by the wall between two large potted plants. Jasmine took her compact out of her handbag and checked her lipstick. Hair could have done with a brush, but it was too late now. "Sit up, Ray," she said sharply. "First impressions and all that."

Ray gave her a look that said he couldn't care less, but he sat up anyway. She liked that about Ray. He probably thought she was a bitch but he had the good manners not to say so out loud, not to her anyway. A striking blonde dressed in a tight miniskirt and almost see-through blouse came out of the lift and walked towards them. Ray straightened up further before standing.

"Armadillo?" she asked as she approached.

"That's us." Ray extended his hand. "Ray Donovan. This is Jasmine Pepper."

Jas stood up and gave the girl her best smile. "I'm the account manager. Ray's my assistant."

"Right-o. I'm Roisin. Max is ready for you now." Irish name, Australian accent.

Roisin led the way to the lift and they ascended to the sixteenth floor. Hierarchy. The higher you were in the company, the higher your office. Jasmine avoided looking out as the lift rose majestically up the outside of the building, its sheer glass walls giving the occupants a fine view of the city. She didn't suffer from vertigo but she wasn't a fan of heights. Her worst nightmare was having to take clients on the London Eye. She had delegated that task to Ray on more than one occasion. He grinned at her knowingly, enjoying her discomfort. *Bastard.* She would make him pay.

Once inside the meeting room, Roisin took their orders for coffee and disappeared. "Nice arse," said Ray as he sat down.

"Behave!"

"You noticed it as well. I saw you looking."

"I was not!"

"You ogled her tits, though." He placed the proposal documents on the table.

Jas ignored him and took her iPad out of her bag. "Make sure you take good notes," she said to him. Roisin returned carrying a tray with coffee in china cups and a selection of biscuits on a plate. They settled down with their drinks, Ray helping himself to two biscuits. He knew Jas wouldn't be having one.

The door opened again and another woman entered. She was the antithesis of Roisin, the buxom, tanned, blonde surfer girl. Tall, slender, short brown hair, smart business suit, the newcomer was the epitome of a successful city executive. Jas tried not to breathe heavily. Her research hadn't been good enough. This was obviously the marketing director, Max Fleetwood. Roisin carefully placed a black coffee in front of her boss as she sat down at the head of the table.

"So, Ms Pepper, what have you got for us?" It was a soft, low-pitched voice, almost accent-less.

Unable to utter a word, Jasmine passed one of the proposal documents over to her.

Without looking at it, the director passed it across the table to Roisin. "Talk me through it," she said, piercing Jasmine with a clear blue-eyed stare.

The next half hour was the most uncomfortable Jas had ever experienced in her career.

†

Out on the pavement when the ordeal was over, she looked despairingly at her assistant. "I think we've blown it, Ray." She always found dealing with men easy; women were much harder to read. Especially smart high-flyers like Max Fleetwood.

"Oh, I don't know. I think that Roisin likes me."

"She's not the one making the decisions."

"I wouldn't be too sure about that."

Jas stared at him. "What? You don't think she and Max are an item?"

Ray flagged down a taxi and waited until they had settled into their seats before replying. "There were looks passing between them. You probably didn't notice, too busy trying to make an impression on her highness."

"Yeah, well, I don't think she was impressed."

The rest of the day passed in a flurry of the usual phone calls, emails and press release deadlines. A text from Den late afternoon said she was meeting the professor at her hotel later. Another reason Jas thought Kathryn wasn't really interested in a serious relationship with her friend. The professor always stayed in a hotel when she came to London and had never spent the night at Den's place, a house she shared with three others. Although, admittedly, Den would need to hire professional cleaners and a team of decorators to make her room look presentable.

She was tidying her desk prior to leaving the office at six thirty when her phone rang. She snatched it up, thinking it would be one of her friends wanting to meet for a Friday night drink. The voice on the other end caught her out completely. "Ms Pepper? Max Fleetwood here."

Jasmine gulped and tried her best to sound professional. "Yes, but please call me Jasmine, or Jas."

"All right, Jasmine."

The sound of Max's sexy tone saying her name made her squirm. *So glad they weren't on Skype or FaceTime.*

"I would like to discuss your proposal in more detail with you," the low voice continued. "Could you meet me for lunch tomorrow?"

"I'll just check my diary." Jasmine's attempt to sound cool wouldn't have deceived anyone. Even if she had an engagement with the Queen, she wasn't going to say no.

"Yes, that would be fine," she said after a moment's pause.

"Good. I'll see you at The Ivy at one o'clock." The line went dead.

Jasmine put the receiver down and stared at the phone. Had that really just happened? Max Fleetwood invited her to lunch, at The Ivy. She had only been there for corporate events. It wasn't somewhere she could afford to eat if paying her own way. It was only as she walked down the stairs that she remembered—tomorrow was Saturday.

†

Kathryn's call had set back Den's plans for the evening. It seemed her interview was being continued over dinner. Maybe it was too much to hope that Kathryn would be persuaded to take the London job by being taken out to a posh restaurant by her prospective employers. Her own attempts to sway the professor in favour of the capital on previous visits with expensive meals hadn't made any impression. Still, at least she would be seeing her afterwards and maybe a night of lovemaking would help her make her mind up.

She sat on the wall outside the pub watching the muddy water flow past. The tide was out and the river didn't look very appealing. Den thought of Sarah, a one-time girlfriend, who had belonged to the rowing club nearby. She'd never understood the appeal of rowing down an open sewer. The Thames was cleaner than it had been in previous centuries, but it still wasn't advisable to swim in it. Sarah had been an enthusiastic rower. A bit too much of a fanatic as it turned out. Den couldn't compete with her rigorous training regime.

Time to make a move if she was going to make it to Kathryn's hotel by ten. She returned her empty pint glass to the bar and set off for the Hammersmith tube station. The walk under the flyover was as dismal as ever even with the recent makeover. At least the old 'Free Bill Stickers' and 'Bill Stickers is Innocent' graffiti was gone, along with the original signs 'Bill Stickers will be Prosecuted'. The tube took her into the West End and alighting at Piccadilly Circus meant she only had a short walk to the hotel.

The bar wasn't very busy and she didn't see the professor. It had been a long day for her, so she had probably gone straight to her room. Den took the lift up to the fifth floor. Kathryn had been able to get the same room she'd had before. Knocking lightly, Den waited, hoping she wasn't too early. The door opened just as she was thinking she would have to wait a bit longer in the bar. Kathryn was wearing a bulky white hotel bathrobe, her hair damp from the shower.

"Hey, babe. You look great." She reached out to touch the wet strands falling over Kathryn's face. Without her glasses, her pale blue eyes had an unfocused look.

"Come in, you idiot," she said, backing up to let Den in.

"Did you think I was the maid bringing more towels?"

"No. She's already been." Kathryn continued walking into the bedroom.

Den's eyes followed her. Even in the oversized robe, her movements were sexy. She experienced the familiar jolt of desire that characterised any meeting with Kathryn. The older woman made her feel like a hormonal teenager, out of control, raw with need.

"Kat?" She wanted her now. "What happened? Did they offer you the job?"

Kathryn had opened the mini bar. "What do you want to drink?" she asked.

Den closed her eyes and hoped this night wasn't going to turn out to be a damp squib. "A lager, if there is one," she said, trying not to sound annoyed. She waited impatiently while Kathryn fixed herself a gin and tonic and opened a bottle of Becks for her. Taking her drink and sitting down in the chair by the window, the professor finally looked at her.

"They've made an offer."

"Kat, you're killing me." Den sipped at the lager she didn't really want. "Are you going to take it?"

"I'm thinking about it."

"Only thinking?" Den wanted to hurl the bottle across the room and shake Kathryn up.

"Well, it's a big move for me, if I take it. Where would I live, for a start?"

"You could stay with me for a bit, until you find somewhere."

"What? In that squat you call home?"

"You've never been. It's not that bad. Anyway, you'll be lucky to find anywhere closer to the uni, at a decent price."

"See, that's what I mean. If I go with the Durham offer, it won't be much of a change. I can afford a house nearby, almost in the country, but within easy commuting distance. Or maybe even a flat near the university. It would be healthier to be able to walk to work. To even buy my own house down here I'd have to live a hundred miles out and spend a fortune on train fares."

"Brighton's only fifty miles away."

"I don't want to live in Brighton."

"Is that the only reason you can come up with for not taking this job?"

Kathryn had found her glasses and put them on. She looked across at Den. "I think it's a good one." The robe had fallen open giving Den a good view of the professor's well-shaped legs. Her eyes travelled up to the tantalising glimpse of bushy hair, a slightly darker colour than the hair on her head. She swallowed, taking another sip of the now tepid beer.

"Great. Just great. I thought maybe I meant more to you than the occasional fuck. Jas is right. I don't know why I put up with this." Without waiting for a response, Den slammed out of the room. Checking her phone as she left the building she realised it was probably too late to call on Jas and she didn't feel like hitting a club either. Fighting back the tears that were threatening, she made her way down the steps of the tube station. Might as well join the other late Friday night travellers on their journeys into the dark. The first train to come along was a District Line one so she jumped on. The walk from the Ravenscourt Park station wasn't as picturesque as her preferred ramble by the river, but safer at this time of night.

She kept checking her phone. No messages. No missed calls. Well, Kathryn really didn't care, did she? Turning the corner into the street, she was relieved to see no lights on. Good, she wasn't going to have to speak to anyone.

Her room was as she'd left it earlier in the day. Bed unmade, clothes in a heap by the window, newspapers everywhere. She was such a slob, how could she even imagine Kathryn wanting to live with her? She collapsed onto her bed and fell asleep immediately, overcome by the exhausting overflow of emotions.

†

Sleep hadn't come easily. Kathryn kept going over the events of the day. She had been pleased to see Den when she arrived at the train station. Their lunch had been enjoyable and she cherished the anticipation of their sexual encounter later. Then there was the interview at the university followed by a tour of the facilities. It was a large department and really did offer her the best opportunity to develop her field of study and research projects. The dinner had been an undisguised attempt to give her a chance to get to know some of her prospective new colleagues. They were pushing hard for an answer. Almost as hard as Den. Why did she keep pushing her away? Was she afraid of the younger woman's intensity? There was only an eight-year age difference, but sometimes it felt like twenty. At least with Ellie, she felt she was on equal terms. No, she couldn't go there anymore. Ellie had made her choice clear; although why she picked the feckless Robin over her she would never know.

Waking early, she spent more time tossing and turning. Her train back to Leeds wasn't until three. When she planned this trip she had thought the morning would be spent in bed with Den. Finally, giving in, she got up and checked the hotel's restaurant guide. Breakfast not served until eight on Saturdays. She could order room service. Or, she could go out and find a café open somewhere—she was in the big city after all.

Getting dressed, she caught sight of herself in the mirror. What did Den see in her? The lack of sleep made her feel like a frumpy fifty-two-year-old, fifty-three this year. She remembered the hurt in Den's voice the night before and wondered why she hadn't at least called her.

There was something she could do. Den was right. She had never seen where she lived. The business card Den had given her when they first met was still in the inside pocket of her briefcase. She noted the address and feeling suddenly more positive, Kathryn collected all her belongings and made her way down to reception. Settling the bill, she walked out onto the street and hailed the first passing taxi. It was a longer journey than she'd expected. Her knowledge of London only revolved around visits to the British Museum and the university. She was vaguely aware that Chiswick was to the west but she had thought it was just past Kensington.

The sight of the smart terraced houses the taxi left her at was a surprise. She had expected to be dropped off at one of the seedy-looking terraces they passed en route. This street close to the river was much more suburban looking than she thought it would be. The way Den dressed and acted, Kathryn really did think she lived in a less refined area.

16

It was only seven thirty, but she decided to take a chance that one of the occupants would be up and about. The door-bell sounded a chime in the hallway. The door was opened by a young man, late thirties she would have guessed, smartly dressed in a neatly pressed button-down white shirt and light-coloured chinos, not too different from her own outfit.

He looked at her enquiringly, probably thought she was canvassing for the local elections. "Hi. Sorry to bother you. Is Den in?"

"Um. Yes, I think so." He smiled suddenly. "You must be Kathryn. I'm Henry. Please, do come in."

Kathryn followed him down a hallway to a bright kitch-en at the back of the house. French windows opened out onto a small well-kept garden. The smell of freshly brewed coffee hit her nostrils.

"Paul and I were just going to have breakfast. Would you care to join us?"

"Yes, that would be lovely. Thank you."

"Please, have a seat." He indicated the kitchen table, which was set for two.

Den hadn't told her anything about her housemates. She would have suspected a less conventional household. The kitchen she found herself in had all the trappings of a televi-sion chef's dreams. Henry bustled about, setting a place for her, and placing a very welcome cup of coffee in front of her. "Den's not likely to surface for a while yet," he said as he started to scramble eggs.

"How did you know who I was?" she asked.

"Not hard to guess. She talks about you a lot. And we've read about you, of course."

Of course. Last year's excavations at Starling Hill had made headline news with the feature articles written by Den. "So, you have me at a disadvantage. I don't know anything about you."

17

"Well, I'm hurt. That's her off my Christmas card list."
He gave her a camp flip of his wrist, and then turned his attention back to the eggs.

Another young man appeared from the garden. "Got a few chives, but we've finished the parsley. Hello!" He stopped to look at Kathryn. "Oh my! It's Dr Moss, isn't it?" He dropped the handful of chives on the counter next to Henry and extended his other hand towards her. She took it and nodded. "I'm Paul. I guess you've met Henry. So, to what do we owe the pleasure?" He helped himself to coffee from the pot and sat down in the chair opposite.

"Den and I had a bit of a fallout last night. I thought I should see her before heading home."

"Ah, right. Do you want me to go and wake her up?"

"No. I mean…there's no rush. My train doesn't leave until three."

"Great. So, tell us, how did it feel when you first realised who was buried at Starling Hill?"

"Paul!" Henry placed a plate of perfectly scrambled eggs with brown toast on the side in front of her. "Let the poor woman eat before you start grilling her. Please go ahead, Kathryn. I'll just do our toast."

Kathryn realised she was very hungry. She was halfway through her eggs by the time Henry sat down with his own plate.

"These eggs are wonderful," she said. "Do you get them locally?" Only after she asked did she think that was probably a stupid question. She wasn't in the country now.

"Well, as local as anything around here. They're supposedly farm fresh."

"Free range," added Paul.

They were a handsome couple, Kathryn thought. Paul was more casually dressed, wearing cut-off denim shorts and a tank top that showed off his pecs. "You'll have to fill me in on what you two do, as Den has told me nothing about you."

"I'm a pilot," Henry said. "Long-haul flights, so it's a treat to be home for a few days now."

"And I'm a kept man," said Paul, lightly.

"Hardly." Henry smiled fondly at him. "He's a ward nurse at St Thomas's."

"Isn't there another person living here, apart from Den, that is?"

"Oh, yeah. Steph. She's a gardener. Must tell her we need more parsley. Anyway, she shot off to Brighton after work yesterday. Somebody's fortieth birthday bash, I think."

Paul started again, gently quizzing Kathryn about last year's dig. They both seemed interested so she humoured them and talked easily about the excavation and the main findings. "The skeletons will be on show at the British Museum later this year," she told them. "An exhibition is being prepared. Finally some recognition for the Queen of the Brigantes."

They had all enjoyed a second round of coffee when Den appeared in the doorway wearing only a scruffy T-shirt and black boxer shorts. Her hair was standing on end and Kathryn's heart lurched at the sight of her lover's long limbs on display.

"I could murder a coffee, Hen!" She stopped, seeing Kathryn staring at her. "Oh, Christ!" Her cheeks flamed and she turned on her heel. They heard her thumping back up the stairs.

Kathryn bit her lip. She stood up. Paul put a restraining hand on her arm.

"I think she might need a bit of time."

"I have seen her looking worse."

Henry laughed. "It's her bedroom she's concerned about. If she wasn't expecting a royal visit, it'll be a tip."

She sat back down and leant back in her chair. Now that the time had come she wasn't sure what she was going to say to Den. With all the excitement of the past year, the excavation, the discoveries, the constant requests for talks, as well as her ongoing responsibilities at the university, she hadn't really thought about the implications of moving. Her house in Lindley, a leafy part of Huddersfield, was all she had ever wanted in a home. The idea of uprooting was suddenly more frightening than appealing. A new location would mean having to register with a new doctor, dentist, and finding a hairdresser she liked. Was she really prepared to go through all that at her age? Another voice in her head was saying, 'go for it, you only live once.' And that was a philosophy she had always promoted.

"Would you like help with the dishes?" she asked Henry as he began to clear the plates.

"No, definitely not. Den's room is on the top floor, just follow all the stairs up." He seemed to have sensed her anxiety.

"Okay. Thanks for breakfast. It was absolutely delicious. Much better than I would have got at the hotel."

"Go on!" He poured another mug of coffee. "And take this up. She's not worth talking to until she's had a hit of caffeine."

Kathryn smiled at him and took the mug. She followed the stairs up to the top of the house. No wonder Den was in good shape if she climbed these several times a day. The door had a hand-painted porcelain sign on it. Den's Den. Cute, but not quite the image she had of her lover.

Pausing to catch her breath, Kathryn raised her hand to knock.

†

Jasmine woke in a sweat. She had been dreaming. A highly charged erotic dream and for the first time in over a year, the face of her lover wasn't Robin. She sat up and tried to recapture the rapidly fleeing images. Max Fleetwood. The lunchtime meeting. Not for the first time since last evening's phone call, she wondered, did the woman really want to discuss the PR proposal or was this a date? Jas licked her lips and checked the time on her phone.

Ten fifteen. Damn! She struggled out of the damp sheets. Just time to have a shower, slap on some makeup and decide what to wear. Her flat was in one of the few areas with a London postcode that wasn't on a tube route. She was at the mercy of the Saturday bus schedules. Making it down to the Theatre District in time to meet Max at The Ivy for one o'clock would be pushing it unless she got a move on. And she had the feeling Ms Fleetwood would not be impressed if she was even a minute late.

†

Den opened the door. Unsmiling, she stood aside to let Kathryn enter. She had hastily thrown on the jeans she'd been wearing the night before and tidied the rest of the clothing on the floor into the laundry basket. Newspapers were now piled up in the corner by her desk and a quick flick of the duvet made the bed look more respectable. She had just opened the window when Kathryn knocked. Glancing around she decided it would have to do.

Kathryn handed her a mug of coffee. "Henry thought you might need this," she said.

"Too right," Den muttered. She watched the professor over the rim of the mug as she glanced around the room, assessing the size of the mess that constituted Den's life.

"I guess I should have phoned."

"Yeah."

"Mind if I sit down? Those stairs are a killer."

"Fine. Make yourself at home." Den realised, belatedly, that she hadn't combed her hair.

"The boys seem nice."

"Yeah, they are." Sipping at her coffee, Den tried to work out what Kathryn was trying to say. The shock of seeing her in the kitchen was fading and being replaced with the anger of the night before.

Kathryn looked up at her. She had chosen to sit on the bed. "Den, I'm sorry. Last night, I was…I don't know. This isn't like me. I just don't know whether I'm doing the right thing." Tears were now streaming freely down her face.

Den put her mug down and sat next to her. This wasn't a Kathryn she knew. The professor was always so much in control of her emotions. Softening, she put her arm around the crying woman's shoulders. "Hey, come on." She reached over and removed Kathryn's glasses. "I'm sorry too. I guess I've been putting pressure on you."

Feeling Kathryn slowly relax against her chest, her breathing calming, Den moved a hand to lift her face up to hers. She kissed her closed eyes first, tracing the salty tear tracks down her wet cheeks. Their lips met and Kathryn's parted to let her explore with her tongue. The professor's moans encouraged Den to move her hands down to her breasts.

Several hours later, both naked and sexually sated, Kathryn glanced at the time on the clock by the bed. "I guess I'm going to miss my train," she said.

"Do you need to go back today?"

"No. I might be tempted to stay the night."

Den grinned at her. "What, in this squat?" she asked playfully.

"It's a nice house."

"I would have cleaned up if I'd known you were coming," Den said more seriously.

Kathryn reached up and tugged at her hair. "I'm glad you didn't. It's just you."

With no further encouragement needed, Den rolled over on top of her and pinned her to the bed. "Well, if you're not going anywhere, how about another round?"

"Have some respect for these old bones."

Den kissed her deeply before answering. "I have every respect for your bones, Professor."

Chapter Two

Agendas

Monday morning and, not for the first time that year, Jasmine didn't feel like going in to work. The falsity of it all and the type of person she had become was finally making an impact on her. She just didn't believe in making up reasons for people to buy things they didn't either want or need. It was getting harder to motivate herself and, since the bosses had decided to make cuts, which meant junior managers no longer had the luxury of a company car, her dissatisfaction with the job deepened each day that she had to use public transport to get to work.

The pavement was slick from the rain and she thought about going back and changing into trainers before she reached the end of the road. But then she wouldn't have time to slip into her favourite Starbucks on the way to the office. The idea of coffee while seated comfortably out of the rain watching the world pass by won out and she continued, carefully, on her way.

Feeling more cheerful with each sip of the flat white, she reviewed her meeting with Max Fleetwood on Saturday. Something about the woman made her feel incredibly sexy. They had talked about the proposal over lunch. And towards the end, Max had said, "Roisin will be your liaison."

Jas squirmed in her seat as she recalled her response. "I would prefer to liaise with you."

Max had given her a penetrating look that bored right into her. "Be careful what you wish for."

And now, she wondered, what was she wishing for? Another meeting with Max, on whatever pretext she could dream up? It would have to be something more credible than just changes to the proposal. Max had made it clear that Roisin would see the first drafts and artwork mock-ups before anyone else.

✝

Kathryn felt the train move out of the station. It was the early morning train out of King's Cross and if it ran to time she could be in her office by ten thirty. Opening her eyes, she decided she might as well make good use of the next few hours rather than dwelling on the last two days, and nights, with Den. Not that they had spent the entire time in bed. Henry had cooked a wonderful meal Saturday night and they joined him and Paul for the evening. It had been relaxing and fun. And on Sunday, they had made it out of bed in time to go for a pub lunch and a walk by the river. She knew Den was making the effort to show her that living in London wasn't such a bad idea.

Rubbing the last remnants of sleep out of her eyes, Kathryn adjusted her glasses and reached for her laptop. She smiled then, as she pulled the small plastic tub out of her briefcase. A slice of Henry's homemade apple pie was nestled inside. The handwritten note taped on top said simply, *Come back soon!* with the letter H encircled by a heart. She didn't know when he'd managed to slip that in. Perhaps when they were waiting at the door for the taxi and Den was holding on to her as if her life depended on it.

She had certainly seen a different side of Den during the weekend. With Henry and Paul, it was a family atmosphere, and a loving one. Before, when they met only in hotels, she had thought her lover just went back to a lonely bedsit. The kind of shared accommodation she remembered from her student days with piles of unwashed dishes in the sink, arguments over who would clean the oven or the bathroom, and having to label food so the other residents didn't consume it—although they often did anyway.

There was a softer side to Den she didn't often let the rest of the world see. She hid behind her shades and a tough reporter persona. The last two days had been wonderful but Kathryn couldn't afford to dwell on it. There was the paper to prepare for next week's public lecture at the Town Hall. Although she could talk about Cartimandua and the Starling Hill excavation without notes, she wanted to be prepared for the close to sold-out crowd the organisers had told her about.

And then there was Durham. She hadn't told Den that she was leaning towards the offer from the northern university. It was only a two-hour drive from Huddersfield in a part of the country she loved, not far from Hadrian's Wall as well as the wonderful walking countryside of the North Yorkshire Dales. Even though it was designated a city, due to having a cathedral, it was smaller than Huddersfield and the university's archaeology department was rated as one of the best in the world. Although the facilities at the London university were impressive, and the faculty members she'd met seemed like people she could work with, she wasn't convinced that city life would suit her in the long-term.

†

Sitting in her office later that day, Kathryn contemplated the framed picture above her desk. It was a beautifully composed photograph of the golden torque found with Queen

Cartimandua's bones at Starling Hill, symbolic of the queen's wealth. The meagre haul of valuable items in the grave indicated that the queen left her royal position in a hurry. No longer in favour at court, she may have had to do a moonlight flit with her lover, just taking what could be carried on horseback.

Whenever she spoke in public about Cartimandua, Kathryn tried to give a positive spin on her life. Historians hadn't been kind to her; she had been labelled 'the traitor queen'. Yet she had ruled over the largest tribe in Britain for a long time. She was already in power at the time of the AD43 invasion and wasn't ousted by her husband until AD69. Twenty-seven years accounted for and she must have already been established as the tribal chief when the Romans started arriving in numbers in 43. Her role as a peacemaker was glossed over. Other tribes suffered great loss of life and land while the Queen of the Brigantes was keeping her people safe. Her achievements were overshadowed by Boudica's revolt. Even in academic circles, the Iceni leader's uprising was seen to symbolise the true British spirit—the fierce desire to repel all invaders.

She checked her phone. One missed call—Den. Maybe later. For now she needed to concentrate on her notes.

†

The raindrops chased each other down the window as Den watched puddles form on the patio. Kathryn's taxi had gone and she wasn't sure how she was going to cope. Saying goodbye had been harder this time. Holding her tightly as they waited by the door for the taxi to arrive, Den had whispered into her ear, "I'll miss you." Kathryn had murmured an inaudible response. And then she was gone. Now it was just the rain and her tears falling in unison.

An arm reached around her waist and held her close. Henry, she knew by the aftershave. And the white sleeve of his uniform shirt meant he would be leaving soon as well.

"Hey, it's not the end of the world. She'll be back."

"And how do you know?" Den sniffed.

"She loves you."

"Did she tell you that?" Den turned and looked at him. "She's never said it to me."

"She doesn't have to. Look, if she didn't care, she would have just gone home Saturday, straight from the hotel. Instead, she came here. She wanted to be with you."

"Yeah. For a weekend of sex. And then she's off back up north and she'll have forgotten me by the time the train has passed Watford."

"True love will find a way."

"Is that how you pass the time on your way to Hong Kong, reading slushy romance novels?"

"Of course. Stops me from falling asleep. Anyway, I'll be back Thursday." He picked up his pilot's case, squeezed her arm and pecked her on the cheek. "Stay out of trouble, and don't forget to eat." His footsteps receded down the hallway.

Den pressed her forehead against the glass as she heard the front door open and close. Four days without Henry. Paul was okay, but she didn't have the same rapport with him. She and Henry had almost grown up together. He was like a younger brother. Their houses were two doors apart when their parents lived in Hampstead. Although Henry was a year younger they had bonded almost immediately and hung out together. Tall for her age, Den was able to outrun him and reach the lower branches of trees to climb, hauling him up like a sack of potatoes. With their birthdays only a week apart, they had started combining parties by the time they were twelve and thirteen.

The other lodger in the house was Steph, who Den didn't know well. Their hours didn't mesh. Steph, working as a self-employed gardener, was up and out of the house early in the morning, whereas Den was a late riser.

It was early now, too early to start work. Den climbed the stairs, feeling suddenly weary. The last two days had been amazing and she'd been on a high throughout. Now she was down, on the lowest of a low, wondering when she would hear from Kathryn again.

†

Friday night at last. Jasmine had been in a heightened state of excitement all day. In fact, she'd felt that way ever since the call from Max on Wednesday morning inviting her to join her for dinner at her house. She had said they would be going out to a club afterwards as well.

Jas spent the next few days going through her wardrobe trying to decide what she should wear. An intimate evening with Max Fleetwood was more than she could have hoped for after the pathetic performance she had put on at the PR campaign presentation the week before. Still, she must have impressed Max at their Saturday lunchtime meeting. Dinner at her house in Kensington was definitely a step up from her usual dates.

Her parents worried about her single status. She was an only child and she knew they were disappointed she had reached the ripe old age of forty-five and no sign of grand-children. They hadn't entirely given up hope and her visits home usually involved having to fend off the attentions of a single male they had rustled up in an attempt to get her respectably married off. Visiting her parents often felt like stepping into a Jane Austen novel.

It was ridiculous, at her age, that she still feared coming out to her parents. Why was she afraid of upsetting her moth-

29

er's bridge circle or her father's golfing buddies? Most of her work colleagues knew she was gay but it wasn't something she discussed with them. It just wasn't an issue, an advantage of living in the big city. There were times when she wished she could be as laid-back as Den about her sexuality.

Den's family had been supportive as soon as they knew. And, in typical Den fashion, she had just brought her girl-friend at the time to a family party and introduced her, and they had accepted the fact without fuss. Den's attitude was generally, 'Fuck 'em. If they don't like it, it's their problem, not mine.' It was a sentiment she agreed with, but somehow couldn't translate into her dealings with her own parents.

Perhaps they would approve of Max when they met her. She was, after all, the embodiment of the type of man they wanted her to marry. So why should a little matter, like her gender, bother them?

The warmth of the summer-like evening helped her de-cide on slipping into the Aztec-style sundress she'd bought in the Jaeger sale. Her standby black stiletto-heeled sandals and black clutch bag completed the ensemble. She generally fa-voured large hoop-style earrings but she thought the fake di-amond studs were a better fit with the outfit in tandem with the discreet pearl necklace her mother had bought her for her twenty-first birthday. Classy, she thought, as she twirled in front of her full-length mirror. Only the best for a night at the posh end of town.

Feeling like a member of the royal family, she stepped out into the hazy sunlight and seated herself carefully in the back seat of the taxi.

†

Another missed call from Den. Kathryn stared at the phone and shook her head. There was no way she could give her the news over the phone. The week had seemed long, with all the students gone home for the summer and just piles of dissertations to read through and assess. Her only human contact had been with her colleague in the next office, Ed McLaughlin. His osteo-archaeology expertise had helped her enormously with the finds at Starling Hill and she valued his friendship. However, their last conversation had been an uncomfortable one.

"The Dean's worried about student numbers. We're oversubscribed for next term's cohort, but she thinks they will drop out in droves if you go." He left it unsaid that he would miss her.

Kathryn had been avoiding the dean for the last two weeks, hoping she could stay below the radar. Although it was common knowledge in the department that she was considering offers, she wasn't going to give her notice until she had signed the contract with Durham. She was making the trip up north to finalise details at the weekend that included a visit to the university-sponsored dig at Binchester. She would be close to a number of ongoing Roman site excavations, which was another reason for taking the job. The dig at Starling Hill had reminded her how much she loved getting her hands in the soil.

Her phone rang, jolting her out of past reminiscences. The voice on the other end was one she was looking forward to putting some distance between.

"What is it, Aimee? You're not usually still here at this time on a Friday afternoon."

"No need to be rude, Kat." The HR admin assistant knew how to push her buttons and calling her 'Kat' was the one most likely to rile her. Their brief affair was something she deeply regretted. The woman was twenty-three years younger, which wouldn't have mattered if they'd had anything remotely in common. What had she been thinking?

"So, what do you want?" Kathryn had long since decided it was pointless being polite to Aimee.

"You haven't completed your summer leave form. The deadline was last Friday."

"You'll have it Monday."

"What's the problem? It's not that difficult for you professor types with all the leave you have."

"I'm finalising details on a dig." *Not entirely untrue.*

"Okay. But if it's not in my inbox by Monday lunchtime, I'll have to come and collect it personally." The seductive tone of the young woman's voice oozed through the phone line.

"Fine. You'll have it." Kathryn slammed the receiver down, annoyed with herself for letting Aimee get to her, again. Glancing at the clock on the wall she realised it was time to leave. She could be booked into her hotel by five if she left now. There would be time to have a good walk around, have dinner and prepare herself for the next morning's meetings at the university.

She gathered together her papers and shoved them in her briefcase. Giving the Queen's torque a lingering look, she whispered, "Going north, back to your roots, babe."

"Talking to yourself. Bad sign, that."

Kathryn looked around, startled. "Christ's sake, Ed! Couldn't you knock first?"

He grinned at her. "Nah, it's more fun seeing you jump." He looked at her over his glasses before adding in a quieter tone, "So, is this it, then? I'd wish you good luck, but I really don't want you to go."

They had talked about it many times over the past few months. She had asked Ed if he didn't fancy a change too. But it was more complicated for him. He had two school-age kids and didn't want to move them away.

"It's not that far. And I'm sure we'll meet up at conferences." She gave him a brief hug. "Anyway this isn't goodbye yet. I'll be back Monday."

They moved out into the hallway together and she locked her door. "Have a good weekend. Hugs to Elise and the kids." She walked down the hall and a feeling of lightness engulfed her as she approached her car. It was the right decision, at the right time.

✝

Den looked around the sparsely furnished room. No books anywhere. What had she let herself in for? The idea of a casual shag with this woman had seemed like a good idea an hour ago when they were dancing at the club.

A few beers, music, flashing lights, it hadn't taken much to get in the mood, trying to recapture the carefree self who had revelled in nights like this. That was before she met Kathryn. And now, a Friday night, five days since Kathryn left on the early morning train, and she'd only had one short text from her. Den had tried to ring her but always got the answering service. She'd left messages, but nothing. It was as if the Saturday and Sunday before hadn't happened.

Now, in this stranger's house, hearing the toilet flush, the initial flash of desire left as quickly as it had appeared. She knew she couldn't do this; it would just be going through the motions. Not fair to Lindy or Lucy, or whatever her name was. *Shit.*

A vision emerged from the bathroom. The woman looked pretty hot, stripped down to her underwear. A lacy black bra barely containing full, rounded breasts, and skimpy panties that covered even less of her mound of luscious-looking dark curls. Den could feel her body responding. She licked her lips.

"Look, I'm sorry, Lindy. But I can't do this."

"It's Libby. What's the matter, babe? Don't you like what you see?" she arched her back provocatively.

"Sure. I like it a lot. But I have to go." Den backed towards the door.

"You're fucked up! You know that?" Libby's full bottom lip trembled.

"Yeah, I know." There was no graceful way to make her exit. "Maybe some other time. Bye."

She stumbled out onto the street, not even sure where she was. They'd been glued to each other's lips in the taxi ride from the club. Pulling out her phone, she clicked onto the map. Google would help her out.

Walking to the end of the road, she found her location before the phone app did. It wasn't far from Henry's. *Christ, I hope I'm not going to run into Libby in one of my locals any time soon.*

✝

Just walking up the road to Max's house was a thrill. This was a part of London she could only dream about living in. Her parents had helped her pay the deposit on her small garden flat in Stoke Newington and she was still paying off the mortgage ten years later.

She stopped outside the large white Georgian house, the engorged purple flowers of the climbing wisteria vine hanging lusciously over the front door. Taking a deep breath, Jas lifted the brass knocker but the door opened before it fell back in place.

"Ms Pepper. Please come in." The speaker was dressed in a maid's outfit, although a more risqué version than any worn by those employed at nearby royal palaces. When the maid turned to lead her down the hall, Jas got a view of the young woman's bare cheeks. She swallowed nervously. What was she letting herself in for?

Max was leaning against the fireplace in the large sitting room where the scantily-clad maid had taken her. The sight of her hostess looking imposingly handsome dressed in a close-fitting tuxedo dispelled her misgivings. Whatever this evening was leading to, it was likely to be more fun than a lonely night in front of the telly watching repeats of *Rizzoli & Isles*.

✝

The lights were on in the downstairs sitting room. Hoping to find Henry there to talk to, Den was disappointed to see Steph sprawled in an armchair. The younger woman was in good shape, working out at the gym regularly as well as having a physically demanding job. The gym was where she'd met Henry and when she told him she was looking for a place to live because her current flatmates were moving to Brighton, he had offered her the other spare room in the house. She paid lower rent than Den, mainly because her room was a great deal smaller than Den's attic space, and she took care of the garden.

Den couldn't tell if she was asleep or not with her dark brown hair flopped over the front of her eyes, a contrast to the shaved back of her head. She decided to risk waking her.

"Is Henry still up?"

A shake of the head and a portion of hair moved to the side revealing clear brown eyes. "No. They went to bed a while ago."

Den collapsed onto the sofa.

"Been out on the town?"

"Yeah, bit of a wasted effort." Den didn't really want to go into the details of her failed pickup.

"Must've seen some action."

Den looked down at herself to see if she was missing any items of clothing.

"Lipstick all over your mush."

"Oh." Den fished a tissue out of her pocket and swiped at her face. "That better?"

"Not really, but it should wash off. Oh, by the way, I saw your mate, Jas, tonight."

"How do you know Jas? Oh, yeah, the birthday bash…" She hadn't felt much like celebrating her forty-fifth birthday but Henry had been up for the usual joint celebration and had sent out the invitations before she could tell him not to bother.

"Didn't know she was the sub type. Looked the part, though." Steph was sitting up now and giving Den a hard stare.

"What are you talking about?"

"The club I go to. She was there with this really hot dom. I've seen her around and she's a player. Your mate needs to be careful. Max Fleetwood plays for keeps."

Den took in Steph's outfit for the first time. Close-fitting leather vest, leather trousers and metal belt.

"It's a leather club?"

"Points for observation! Fridays are Fetish nights. Tonight was a mistresses and slaves bash."

Den stared at her. "No offence, Steph, but no way is Jas into anything like that."

"Could've fooled me. Mind you, Max was keeping her on a short leash, obviously not in the mood to share her new acolyte."

This was turning out to be the Friday night from hell. First, no word from Kathryn. Second, trying to score and chickening out. Third, finding out her best friend was into some weird shit. As far as she knew, Jas had never shown any interest in anything other than regular sex before. She remembered Jas's naive wonderment at the range of sex toys on display the time she'd dragged her into the Ann Summers shop just to have a laugh. She'd had to explain what a butt plug was used for, and this to someone over forty who had spent her working life living in London. Den briefly considered asking Steph to take her to the club so she could face off to this Max person. But Jas was old enough to look after herself and if she were enjoying it, she wouldn't welcome Den's interference.

"Look, Steph, do me a favour. If you see Jas at this club again and she looks like she's in trouble, would you look out for her?"

"I wouldn't like to cross Max Fleetwood. But, yeah, if I can help in any way…"

Deciding she couldn't take any more of the evening's disturbances, Den just nodded her thanks and headed up the stairs to the sanctity of her room.

Chapter Three

Discussions

Where the previous week had seemed to drag, this one was moving too quickly, heading relentlessly towards the talk at the Town Hall. Kathryn was familiar with the venue, having sat through a number of graduation ceremonies over the years, but she had never been the focus of attention on the stage. She had always sat in the back of the hall in her academic gown, smiling proudly as her students passed in front of her to receive their well-earned diplomas.

The start of the week had been difficult with interviews, first with the vice chancellor and then the dean. They had both tried to persuade her to change her mind but she had assured them that the Archaeology Department at the university was established enough now to still attract the students they needed to fill the courses. It was a numbers game and that was all they were concerned about.

The vice chancellor wasn't someone she had much contact with so they had parted amicably enough. Her relationship with the dean was another matter, prickly at best. They were too much alike and Ed had pointed out that the dean probably felt threatened by her. But the last thing she wanted was a position at that level. She enjoyed her teaching time and found administrative chores a bore.

And then there was the meeting with the head of HR. She always wondered how it was that people in the farcically named Human Resources seemed the least likely to have the necessary qualities for dealing sensitively with people. It was a most dehumanising experience. She was just pleased to have avoided a face-to-face confrontation with Aimee Felton.

With all that out of the way, she had finally been able to concentrate on preparation for the talk. Unable to make the call herself, she had asked Ed to contact Eleanor Winters to see if she would consider coming along on the evening even though she had known there wasn't much chance of it happening.

Ellie had taught Roman history and was capable of commanding an audience of unruly teenagers. But she had spent the last twenty years creating pottery and led a reclusive lifestyle. Although interested in the finds made on her property, she had found the events of the previous summer disturbing. And since her marriage to Robin, well, Kathryn didn't want to even go there, but thoughts of Ellie intruded just the same.

Ed walked in on her as she was contemplating what might have been. He shrugged. "Yes, I spoke to her. She was aware of the talk, of course, but she said she has no intention of going. She lived through it."

"Okay, I guess I expected that." Kathryn sighed.

"She did say, though, that she would appreciate it if you could emphasise that the field has been re-turfed and there is nothing to see at Starling Hill. She doesn't want a repeat of last summer with another media circus."

"Of course, I was going to say that."

"And she also thinks you should say there's no more bling to be found. She doesn't want to be over-run with hordes of amateur metal detectorists. I suspect there will be a fair sprinkling of locals in the audience, some of her neighbours. They will, no doubt, be concerned about the same thing."

"Okay, Ed. I get the message."

He continued to block her doorway. She looked up at him.

"So, do you have a leaving date?"

"It's not cut-and-dried. I have some leave to take before the end of August. Then I'll be going up to Durham to sort out my teaching and tutoring schedules. I've agreed to come back for the grad ceremonies in November because it's always a thrill to see my students graduate."

"What about your PhD group?"

She still had three students going for their doctorates. "I will see each of them personally before I leave, probably off campus. And I'm not a million miles away if they need to contact me before their vivas. They're all understandably nervous about the oral examination, although I think they will be fine."

"Well, I'm in charge of organising your leaving do. So, when do you think you can fit us in?"

"Oh, come on, Ed. You know I hate that sort of thing."

"There aren't that many of us. It'll just be like going out for a drink with a few mates and I promise not to breathe a word to the HR department."

Kathryn sighed. It would be just like Aimee to invite herself along. "I think we should have it out of town somewhere. Newcastle might be far enough away."

Ed laughed. "That might work." He started to walk away. "Text me with a date," he called over his shoulder.

†

"She's not answering my calls. I've left messages, sent texts. All I've had from her is one measly text since last Monday." Den paced around the kitchen while Henry calmly chopped vegetables for the stir-fry he was making. He slapped her hand away as she tried to nab a piece of celery.

"Have you got anything on this week?"

"No. I finished subbing that article on Richard. It's going to print now." Ever since her success with the Starling Hill features the previous year, she was in demand for anything to do with archaeology. The decision to have Richard III's remains interred at Leicester rather than York had finally been made, much to the dismay of the Yorkists. Den's article had covered another group's position on the argument, the idea that as a king of England his final resting place would be Westminster. But that wasn't likely to happen as Shakespeare had so successfully blackened his name.

"Then do something positive." Henry started on the carrots. "Go up there and find out what's going on with her."

"I can't just turn up on her doorstep like some pathetic lovesick puppy."

"So, what's the option? You continue to mooch around here like a lovesick puppy?"

Den grabbed a piece of carrot and started chewing on it. Henry sighed and put down his knife.

"Call yourself a journalist? Where's your laptop?"

"On the table."

"Okay. Fire it up and do a search on her name."

"Do you know how many Kathryn Moss's there are?"

"Geez. What did your last researcher die of? Put in Huddersfield or archaeology professor, or Starling Hill even."

Den finished the carrot and opened up her MacBook Air. The search didn't take long. She looked up at Henry. "Did you already know about this?"

"Might have."

"You bastard."

"Just thank me for trying to salvage your love life." He opened another drawer and pulled out an envelope. "Start packing. Your train leaves at two tomorrow."

She opened the envelope and looked at the contents. "This is a one-way ticket."

"I'm an optimist."

"Henry Stamer! Have I ever told you I love you?"

"Sure, but save the mushy stuff for the professor."

†

Den stood on the steps outside the train station looking out on the expanse of wet pavement, the back of the Harold Wilson statue. She recalled the last time she had seen this view. Kathryn had abandoned her here. She'd been at a loss, never having been to Huddersfield before. Luckily there was a hotel on the square and she had been able to book a room. Perhaps Kathryn had never really forgiven her for the theft of her files that first night they slept together. She thought they had gotten past that in their relationship. What relationship, she wondered now? Maybe that initial breach of trust would forever sour what might have been between her and Kathryn.

Den knew from her previous visit that it was only a short walk from the train station to the Town Hall. With time to kill before the lecture started, Den made her way to the bar in the George and settled down to wait. Checking her phone, there was no message from Jas. Great. First Kathryn ignored her, now her best mate. When she had last spoken to her, finally getting through to her at work on Monday morning, Jas had cut her short when she brought up the subject of her Friday night foray into the world of leather (and she wasn't talking sofas). She just said she was fine, it was 'all good' and she would catch up with her later. And the fact was she sounded more cheerful than she usually did on a Monday, so

Den decided to leave it. Jas knew where to turn if she got into trouble.

When it was time to make a move, Den went out into the bright summer evening and walked along the street towards the Town Hall. The sidewalk was almost as crowded as Oxford Street with people coming out of offices and shops, going into restaurants and pubs. She tried to switch into journalist mode, observing everything as she walked. But the knowledge that she was only minutes away from seeing Kathryn made it hard to concentrate. Entering the lobby of the large square building she was surprised at the size of the crowd. The Town Hall, like so many in these northern industrial towns, was an imposing structure. One of the ushers helped her find her seat, which was very near the front. She wondered at Henry's foresight, he must have booked the ticket weeks ago. The way the hall was filling up, including the gallery, it looked like a sell-out. Kathryn was of celebrity status here now, and Huddersfield was well and truly embedded on the archaeological map of the British Isles. Starling Hill had acquired the stature of Holmfirth in people's imagination and that was famous for being the site of the long-running television comedy, *Last of the Summer Wine*.

Henry had thought of everything, even making sure she had an aisle seat so she could stretch out her long legs. Only six rows back from the front she found herself looking up at the stage. There was a lectern set off to one side, but she knew from seeing Kathryn in action at other events that she would move around as she talked. The large screen suspended from the high ceiling barely concealed the huge pipes of the organ looming up against the back wall. Information gleaned on the Internet had informed her that the hall could hold twelve hundred people and was a popular venue for concerts of a wide range of music. There was even a ukulele festival advertised for September.

The lights dimmed and the hum of conversations died down with the occasional cough and sniffle. There was a brief introduction from Dr Ed McLaughlin who Den knew was a close colleague of Kathryn's. She had seen him at the site the year before but hadn't spoken with him. He kept his introductory remarks brief, as he was well aware the audience hadn't come to see him. When Kathryn walked onto the stage there was a big round of applause. The professor waited for the noise to die down, acknowledging the crowd, smiling and glancing around.

The next hour was a torment for Den. She wondered why she had thought attending the lecture would be a good idea. Watching Kathryn as she gave a polished and commanding performance, she was aware only of the heat gathering between her legs and the tight knot in her chest. When the question-and-answer session started it was all she could do to stop herself from jumping up and shouting, *why haven't you answered my calls?*

Ed McLaughlin came out onto the stage again and brought proceedings to a close and the audience rose as one to give Kathryn a standing ovation. The lights went up in the hall and people started to shuffle around looking for bags and jackets. Den stood and stretched her legs. She moved to one side to let the other people from her row out. Her eyes briefly caught Kathryn's as she stopped by the lectern to pick up the notes she hadn't used. Den raised her hand to wave and then let it drop limply to her side as Kathryn turned away without acknowledging her and walked out of view.

A wave of self-pity hit her. Why had she bothered? Tears threatened to fall as she tore her gaze away from the stage and the movement of the crowd carried her out into the foyer.

"Hey, Den! Is that you?"

She turned to face the voice and found herself looking into Robin Fanshawe's hazel eyes.

"Wow, it is you? What brings you this far north without a minder?" Robin was smiling at her, looking as happy and healthy as when Den had last seen her, at her wedding six weeks earlier.

Den swallowed. She wasn't sure she could speak. All she could do was look at Robin and shake her head. The tears were on their way and there was nothing she could do to stop them.

†

Ellie Winters sat on the fence overlooking the field that was now being dug over once again at the Town Hall. The idea of going to Kathryn's talk wasn't one she had entertained for more than a few seconds. She reviewed her conversation with Ed and hoped she hadn't sounded rude on the phone. He didn't deserve to be caught in the middle, and she was angry with Kathryn for putting him in that position.

Nothing could have marred her happiness on the day of the wedding and when she saw the professor there with the journalist, Denise—she thought perhaps Kathryn had finally moved on. But the look on Kathryn's face at the end of the ceremony had only shown pain. She had stiffly wished them both well and quickly moved off to speak to some of her students. When they sent out the invitations she really hadn't thought Kathryn would show up. It just seemed polite to invite her.

The moorland was glowing with the sun making its slow descent towards the horizon. Only a few days to midsummer when she and Kieran would be taking part in the Kirkwood Hospice Midnight Memory Walk, a ten-mile stroll through the streets of Huddersfield with thousands of others. It was an uplifting experience and one they had participated in every year since the death of Kieran's wife to lung cancer. They had missed it last year because Kieran had been in Australia visiting his son and new grandson. When he returned the peace of the farm, along with her life, was in the process of being destroyed.

Thank heavens Kieran Taylor returned when he did. Her longtime pottery mentor and substitute father figure had bonded with Ed McLaughlin immediately, helping the academic with physical tasks like putting up gazebos and moving heavy equipment. Just knowing he was only ten minutes drive away helped Ellie cope with her shifting emotions during the dig. Kathryn was on site every weekday with the students and clearly wanted to renew their previous intimacy. It was a deeply disturbing time. Ellie had asked Robin to leave when two of her lovers turned up at the farm on the same day, Jasmine Pepper and Jo Bright Flame.

Jasmine took off back to London, quick to realise Robin was no longer interested. Jo, on the other hand, wanted to learn how to make pots and Ellie took her on as a student. Over the past year, their initially tentative association blossomed into a firm friendship.

She was happy with her life now but the hopes of putting the less happy memories of the dig behind her were fading as preparations for the Cartimandua exhibition were gaining momentum. This talk of Kathryn's was only the start of what she feared would be more publicity featuring her home.

Ellie had waved Robin off as she headed into town to attend the lecture. Robin said she wanted to make sure the professor adhered to Ellie's request that she mention there was nothing left to see or find at Starling Hill. She roared off down the track on her bike.

Much as she worried about Robin every time she set off on her Harley, Ellie was glad she hadn't been forced to part with it. Their money worries had been eased with the windfall from the value of the burial goods. Not enough to retire on, but it would see them through a few years. She wanted to travel more and had scaled back the pottery production. Artwork was her focus now and she was looking forward to the forthcoming showing of her paintings at a gallery in Hebden Bridge.

Her reverie was disturbed with the sound of the motorbike coming closer. She climbed down from the fence and walked across the yard to greet her lover. Robin had promised her a night of al fresco lovemaking when she returned and Ellie felt a shiver of pleasure run through her at the thought.

As the bike drew closer she realised Robin had a passenger. It seemed their evening's outdoor activity was going to be postponed. Robin brought the bike to a stop by the front door. The visitor dismounted first and removed her helmet.

"Den! What a surprise."

The journalist didn't say anything, just stood looking around in a daze.

"Den's had a bit of a shock. I think we might all need a drink." Robin stowed the helmets away and moved over to Ellie. "Sorry about this, but I couldn't leave her there," she whispered.

"Okay. I think I can find something," Ellie said, leading the way into the house. She went into the kitchen and Robin followed her leaving their unexpected guest in the living room.

Den was staring into the empty grate in the fireplace when they returned. Robin placed a cold bottle of Corona on the table and took a sip from her own. Ellie put a tentative hand on Den's arm. "Come and sit down," she said gently.

While they were in the kitchen Robin told Ellie how Kathryn had ignored Den at the talk. She said Den was incoherent when she questioned her, but gathered that she'd come up from London in the hopes of finding out why Kathryn wasn't answering her calls.

"I didn't see this coming," Robin added. "I didn't think Den was the falling in love type."

"It's been known to happen," Ellie had teased, kissing her lover on the mouth. Robin responded as she knew she would, pulling her close.

Now Ellie steered the distraught journalist to a seat on the couch. Sitting next to her, she said, "I know it's not much comfort, but I don't think she means to be cruel. She just puts things in boxes."

"We had such a good time when she was in London. And that's not even two weeks ago. I thought it meant something. I guess I was wrong." Den sniffed and took a long swallow of cold beer.

"What was she doing in London?" Ellie asked.

"She had a second interview at UCL. I was hoping she would accept their offer but she only said she was thinking about it." Den tipped more beer down her throat.

"Has she had other offers?" Ellie thought this was very likely the case.

"Yeah. Sodding Durham." Den slammed the nearly empty bottle on the table.

"Hmm. Sodding Durham. Do you know where that is, Rob? Somewhere near Chipping Sodbury?" Ellie tried to lighten Den's mood with a bad joke.

Robin didn't respond. She was pacing around the room and had already dislodged Fleur from her favourite position on the back of the armchair. The cat stalked off in disgust.

Ellie knew the reminder that she and Kathryn had once been lovers disturbed Robin. Well, she would have to deal with it. Ellie turned her attention back to Den.

"You haven't spoken to Kathryn since her visit?"

"No. I've left messages. But she hasn't bothered to ring back. I didn't know what to do. For some stupid reason I thought she might be pleased to see me if I came up here."

"Well, she's got a lot on her plate. As well as job interviews she would have had to prepare for this talk." Ellie knew only too well how single-minded the professor could be.

"Fucking hell, she could do this talk in her sleep! The times I've seen her do it, I could do it myself." From Den's angry tone, it was clear she wasn't going to be easily placated.

Robin placed another bottle in front of the journalist. Giving her partner what she hoped was a reassuring look, Ellie tried another tack.

"She didn't expect to see you. When she's had time to think about it she'll realise she reacted badly. Why don't you try phoning her now?"

"Why doesn't she phone me?" Den sounded like a petulant child.

Ellie sighed. Her brief affair with the professor had fizzled out when they stopped communicating. But she hadn't pursued her because she realised the liaison had run its course. Whatever she said now wasn't going to comfort the love struck journalist. "I don't know, Den. She lives in another world, most of the time."

"On another fucking planet, if you ask me," Robin interjected forcefully.

"Robin." Ellie gave her a look that said she wasn't helping. "I'm not sure if I put the hens in for the night. Could you go and check? And see if you can round up Soames. I haven't seen him for a few hours."

"Yeah. All right." Robin sucked down the last of her beer and put the bottle on the table.

†

Robin breathed in the fresh air gratefully. Almost ten o'clock and still light out. She loved this time of year on the farm. Walking slowly over to the chicken run, she was sure she would find they were all safely cooped up. Ellie didn't forget things like that. As for Soames, the large ginger cat was likely out stalking prey in the field. He would turn up in the morning for his bowl of cat food even if he'd already feasted on a vole or two.

Whatever Ellie wanted to tell Den about Kathryn, she didn't want Robin to hear. Even though Robin knew she didn't need to worry about Ellie's connection with the professor, she still felt twinges of jealousy whenever her name came up. She had been surprised to see her at the wedding. But nothing could have spoiled that day for her, even if a legion of Ellie's ex-lovers had arrived. And the fact was, there was no legion, just Kathryn and the woman Ellie had left her husband for, but that was somewhere in the mists of a long-forgotten time. Kathryn was more of a constant presence and her connection with the farm was a permanent feature. People would always know her as the discoverer of Queen Cartimandua's burial place.

Robin had gone to the talk at the Town Hall because she had wanted to see how the professor presented the finds of the previous summer, how much she was using the Starling Hill dig to progress her career. She had to admit that Kathryn was a good presenter and had a compelling story to tell of the deposed queen's last days.

She sat in the upstairs gallery and had a good view of the front of the hall as well as the stage. From her vantage point she had spotted what she thought looked like the back of Denise Sullivan's head but thought she must be mistaken. Why would the journalist venture this far out of her comfort zone to hear a story she had written about many times? The stricken look on Den's face when she called out to her in the foyer was heartbreaking. And Robin knew only too well the feeling. If Kathryn was still carrying a torch for Ellie, Den must be suffering.

The hens were nowhere to be seen. She could hear the gentle clucking noises from the coop indicating they were settled in for the night. She would give it another few minutes before returning to the house. Leaning over the fence facing the field, she wondered where she would be if the dig had never happened. Would she have been given the opportunity to face up to her own past mistakes if the professor hadn't reappeared at that moment in time to ask permission to excavate? Given the chance to start over with Ellie, she had grasped it with both hands. She breathed out slowly. Time to let go. The professor was history—literally.

†

Den looked a bit brighter when she returned to the living room and the bottle in front of her hadn't been emptied.

Ellie looked up. "I was telling Den she can stay here. I changed the sheets after Aiden and Sophie's last visit."

"Yeah. That's good."

"And I thought we could all go into Hebden tomorrow. I'm meeting with Helen about the gallery showing and need to pick up some art supplies. So after you've done your boxing session we can meet up for lunch."

"Sounds like a plan. You okay with that, Den?"

"Sure. I've heard a lot about Hebden Bridge. Is it really the Dykesville of the North?"

"So they say. But don't get your hopes up. All the best looking ones are taken." Robin grinned at her.

†

"What do you mean, she's gone?" Shocked at the sight of Den standing in the auditorium looking up at her, Kathryn asked Ed as soon as she got backstage to see if he could find her. She had a queue of people waiting to ask her questions after the talk ended. Now, they were alone for the first time that evening.

"I saw her leaving with Robin, you know, from the farm."

"Yes, I know who bloody Robin is! Sorry, Ed." Kathryn gave him an apologetic look. "I just didn't expect to see Den here."

"I take it you haven't told her about your move."

"No. I wanted to do it face-to-face. I was planning to go to London next week once this was over and I'd sorted out things with the university."

After making her peace with Ed and agreeing to meet up with him the next day, Kathryn headed home. She was both physically and mentally exhausted.

†

Kathryn took another sip of whiskey. She didn't usually indulge in the hard stuff on a weekday, but she felt the need now. It was either that or knock herself out with sleeping pills. Already hyped up from the talk, she couldn't settle to anything. Every time she closed her eyes she could see the startled look on Den's face. And even more disturbing, the realisation that she was going to have to go to Starling Hill to talk to her.

Sifting through her memories of the weekend in London, she realised that much as she had enjoyed the time spent with Den—the lovemaking, the walk along the river, meeting her housemates—she really hadn't given it any thought once she got back home. She focused on the details of the Durham job, dealing with university admin, and the Town Hall talk. Now that all that was taken care of she could think about her relationship with the journalist. Could it be called a relationship? Den seemed to want some kind of commitment more than she did. But if she were honest with herself, she did enjoy being with her. So, what was the problem?

Was it just a London thing? With the change in the landscape as the train got closer to Leeds, the shape of the hills, the glimpses of empty moorland, London became a distant memory. And as she drove the last few miles towards her home, with the familiar sight of the Castle Hill monument in sight, she knew this was where she belonged. How could she explain that to Den?

Her track record on relationships really sucked, to use the student terminology. How much more time was she going to spend mooning over what she couldn't have and accept the love of someone who did want her? And what was it with these younger women anyway? Aimee Felton was still angling for another date. Den should have little difficulty finding someone her own age in London. So she had her own house, own car, own teeth. Did being an archaeology professor make her a hot dyke sex symbol? In spite of her dark mood, she smiled.

Tomorrow was her last full day at the university and she was planning to remove the remaining files from her office and make sure she left the lab in good shape for her successor. After that, she would make the journey to Starling Hill.

If Den had already gone back to London, she would at least be able to see Ellie.

✝

Den lay awake for a long time. Being back at Starling Hill in these circumstances felt strangely familiar, as it seemed these two were always bailing her out. Robin and Ellie had been on hand to rescue her the previous year when she'd spent a night out on the moors and been shot at by the neighbouring sheep farmer. She smiled at the memory of Robin—a woman she'd never met—ripping off her T-shirt to staunch the blood from where the gunshot wound had grazed her shoulder. Of Robin, leaning over her, bare-chested, and talking to her the whole time. Ellie took over when the air ambulance arrived and travelled with her to the hospital. She already owed them a debt she could never repay. It had been her fault the media had intruded on their peaceful hilltop re-treat. Well, not entirely her fault. Kathryn had started the process by initiating the dig. If she hadn't uncovered the bones, there would have been no media interest. Britain was dotted with Roman remains that didn't generally make front-page news. Without the royal skeleton, Den would have had no story to tell.

In spite of her best efforts, thoughts of Kathryn kept in-truding her mind. By the time she finally drifted off to sleep it was getting light outside.

Waking up in the strange room, hearing unfamiliar sounds, Den tried to make sense of her surroundings. The long narrow windows, the low beamed ceiling, she was at the farmhouse, Starling Hill. Recalling the events of the night before, she sighed heavily and untangled her long legs from under the duvet. Rubbing her eyes she made her way over to the windows and looked out. Robin was in the yard, bent down, talking to a large ginger cat. She smiled. Even if she was unlucky in love, she was fortunate to have good friends. That thought made her realise she should have sent Henry a message. But she didn't want him to be disappointed, for he had gone to a lot of trouble and was only trying to help. Hopefully he would think she was too happily immersed in her reunion with Kathryn to think of contacting him.

Finding the towel Ellie had left out for her, she made her way to the bathroom. A tentative glance in the mirror didn't improve her mood—she looked like crap. The water was hot and she felt marginally better after her shower.

In spite of the cloud cover it was shaping up to be another warm day. She dressed in the surfer shorts and loose-fitting sleeveless top she'd brought. Shoving her feet into her worn sand shoes, she made her way downstairs where a delicious smell of coffee and toast was coming from the kitchen.

✝

Ellie was making scrambled eggs and her taste buds responded. Farm-fresh eggs. Both Robin and the ginger cat were in the kitchen as well. The cat was sitting by an empty bowl watching Ellie through narrowed eyes. Robin was pouring coffee into three mugs. She greeted Den with a smile and handed her a mug.

"Did you sleep okay?"

"Off and on, I guess."

"Well, get some of this down you. Guaranteed to wake the dead. Milk and sugar are on the table."

Den sat down and sipped at the coffee. It was indeed strong. She added milk. Ellie passed over a plate of scrambled eggs on toast. "Thanks. I don't know how I can ever thank you for all this."

"It's just breakfast."

"You know what I mean. You always seem to be rescuing me."

Robin sat down with her own plate of food and mug. "Yeah. We'll be putting a sign up at the end of the lane. Starling Hill Infirmary for Tourists…always wanted a S.H.I.T. acronym."

"Robin!" Ellie sat down opposite her.

"Well, it's true. When I first started living here I was planning to call my web business, Starling Hill I.T. Services, until Ellie kindly pointed out it spelt 'shits'."

Den snorted out some coffee. "No kidding!"

"Yeah. Good thing I moved in with a teacher."

A large paw landed on her thigh. Den looked down at the cat staring back at her with big green eyes.

"Is Soames bothering you?" Ellie looked across the table. "He has been fed but he's rather partial to scrambled eggs. Don't give him any, he's on a diet."

Den gently removed the paw from her leg. "Sorry, mate. But Mum says no." The cat gave her another hard stare before stalking off, tail held high.

"We'll be setting off in an hour. If you want Internet access, Robin can give you the Wi-Fi password." Ellie started clearing plates.

"Hey, leave those, hon. I'm on dish duty." Robin leant over and kissed Ellie between the eyes.

Den felt like an interloper, and the sweetness of the love she was witnessing only increased her sense of despair.

Fifteen minutes later she was sitting at the kitchen table in front of her laptop checking emails. Nothing from Kathryn, but two from Henry. She read the second one twice. There was no way she was going to share her misery with him. She sent a short reply telling him the talk had been great and she was staying for the weekend. He could read into that what he wanted.

She was still staring into space when Robin came in and asked if she could give her a hand. Two of Ellie's large canvases needed lifting into the Jeep. Closing the laptop, she followed her outside.

†

Robin led the way to the studio. It looked very different from her previous visit. Gone were the pottery accoutrements. It had been transformed into an artist's space with spare canvases, brushes, palettes, and the smell of turps.

"Doesn't she do pottery anymore?"

"We've scaled back, just taking orders from existing customers. I had to shut the website down. We were getting all sorts of idiots wanting to come and see the site. The wheel and the kiln are in the other room. Kieran still comes up to fire pots."

The wrapped paintings didn't allow her to see what was on them. "What does she paint?"

"What she knows. The moors, the sky, sheep. Some of her work's been compared to a guy called Constable."

Den looked at her and shook her head. "Guess you're not much of an art connoisseur."

"Nah. I had to look him up. Anyway, people seem to like her stuff. The gallery, where she's having this showing, has already sold two of her pieces. They were smaller than these, though."

"That's impressive. She must be a fast worker."

"Her concentration levels are amazing." Robin's voice was tinged with pride. "Probably comes from years of throwing pots, always aiming for perfection. She's dabbled with paints on and off for years but it was our trip to Italy last year that really inspired her to make a go of it. You know, we haven't even managed to have a honeymoon with all this going on. But it can wait. We'll head off somewhere warm for a few weeks when winter sets in."

They carried the canvases out one by one and placed them carefully in the back of the vehicle. Ellie emerged from the house and announced she was ready to leave when they were. Den followed Robin inside to collect her phone and some cash while Robin picked up her boxing gear.

✝

To Den's surprise it was Ellie who got in the driver's seat of the ungainly off-roader. Robin offered to sit in the back, giving her more legroom and a better view. "And Ellie doesn't like the way I drive," she added, climbing into the back with her gym bag.

Ellie was certainly adept at managing the curves on the narrow lanes in the bulky vehicle. When they arrived in the market town, she was lucky to find a space on the street near the gallery. Robin and Den carried the canvases in, and then Robin took the keys from Ellie and drove off to the boxing gym.

A short, dark-haired woman emerged from the back room. "Ellie!" She gave her a hug and kissed her on both cheeks. "Are these the last two? Wonderful. I have just the space planned out for them." She had a slight accent Den thought, probably French from the way she greeted Ellie.

"Helen, this is Den, a friend from London."

The woman held out her hand. "Pleased to meet you. I was just going next door for a coffee. Would you like to join us?"

"Um, no. Thanks. I'll go for a walk."

"Okay. Well, we'll see you in the White Lion for lunch. It's the big pub next to the old mill, just past the square." Ellie squeezed her arm and smiled encouragingly.

"Fine. I'm sure I'll find it."

✝

The time passed quickly. There were so many interesting little shops. She wandered around and after a short time felt somehow at peace for the first time in the last twenty-four hours. She was thinking of nothing at all while she watched the ducks crowding around the steps by the old bridge and listened to the accordion player busking at the edge of the water. His music had a haunting quality and she was digging change out of her pocket when her phone buzzed. The message was from Robin. *Where r u? We r in pub.*

She quickly texted back, *on steps by ducks.*

Stay there, came back immediately.

She had just thrown some coins into the accordionist's hat when Robin appeared.

"You can't really get lost here," she said, leading the way to the pub.

"Sorry, I lost track of time."

"Did you give that guy money?"

"Yes. Shouldn't I have?" Den asked, suddenly concerned.

"No. I'm glad you did. I've seen him before and he's a good musician. If he weren't genuine the locals would have run him out of town by now. It's a small community."

†

The pub they walked into was another welcoming surprise. Unlike so many of the modernised pubs, it had retained its original features, including a massive stone fireplace, wooden floor, and solid wooden bar. Ellie was already sitting at a table by the wall near the bar sipping from a glass of white wine. There were two glasses of Peroni in front of the two empty chairs.

"We ordered for you. Hope you don't mind," she said, smiling up at her.

"That's great. Thanks." Den sat down and took another deep breath. It was turning out to be a better day than she had expected when she woke that morning.

Robin handed her a menu. "I know what I'm having. The portions here are really big though. Do you want to share a burger?"

"Yeah, that would be good."

"And the chips are made with real potatoes so where it says 'chunky' they mean chunky. And Ellie won't eat hers." She grinned at her partner.

"No. I have to keep my girlish figure. But you two carnivores go ahead. I'll just pick at a lettuce leaf."

Den laughed before she sipped her beer. She was enjoying being with the two newlyweds. They were relaxed with each other and were inviting her into their world.

"What's with all the yellow bike things everywhere?" she asked when their food order had been taken.

"Tour de France. The second stage of the Grand Depart is coming through here in a few weeks." Robin sounded enthusiastic about the event.

"Why here?"

"It's quite challenging for cyclists. In case you haven't noticed, there are some seriously big hills around here."

Throughout lunch they continued an easy conversation with much laughter. When they'd finished eating, Ellie went off to purchase her art supplies and agreed to meet them at the car park in twenty minutes.

†

Robin and Den leant across the bridge watching the water cascading over the weir. "You do know how lucky you are?" Den said after Ellie had left them and was out of earshot.

Robin didn't reply. She just nodded.

They shared a companionable silence for a few more minutes. Den looked over at Robin. "Um, something I want to ask you. It's a bit personal though."

Robin smiled at her. "Go ahead."

"When you were seeing Jas, did you, was she into being you know, submissive?" Den struggled with the words and couldn't help feeling foolish even asking.

Robin didn't look at her when she answered. "I hadn't thought of it like that, but I suppose she did like it rough." She turned to look at her. "Why do you ask?"

"She's seeing someone now who I've been told is a top dom on the scene. Thing is, when I spoke to her she didn't want to talk about it and we've always shared stuff like that."

"Well, maybe this one's important to her. And if it's what she wants she will do anything to get it."

"I know, but I guess it just surprised me. She's never mentioned it before."

"It's all role-play, Den. I wouldn't worry about it." She glanced over at the clock on the building. "Better make a move. Ellie should be ready to go by now."

†

Kathryn finished unloading the last of the boxes from her car. There was nothing more she wanted to do other than collapse on her sofa with a glass of red wine and watch something mindless on the telly. There was probably a World Cup football match on between two countries she couldn't care less about. England was already out of the tournament.

However, she had spent most of the day, as she backed up files, deleted emails, made use of the photocopier for the last time, wondering what to do about Den. She had debated the various methods of communication—email, text, phone, Facebook—but she knew there was really only one. She had to face her in person. And that meant going to Starling Hill. Which meant seeing Ellie again.

The drive up into the hills brought forth mixed feelings. The joys of the previous summer—travelling to the site each day, revelling in the excitement of the daily discoveries that were building into a remarkable story of ancient lives lived— these were the foremost memories overlaid with the emotional turmoil from trying to rekindle her dormant relationship with the farm's owner. As she rounded the last curve on the road leading to the Starling Hill track, she slowed the car down to take in the stunning views again—and to delay her arrival. There was no way of approaching the farm stealthily. Her bright red car stood out against the stark landscape, like a beacon. Anyone standing in the farmyard would see her approach from half a mile away.

She told herself, sternly, to get a grip. She was almost fifty-three years old and a respected university professor, not an inexperienced teenager. Still, reminding herself of her age and professional status didn't make it any easier to do what she had to do.

Taking a deep breath as she parked in front of the farmhouse, she steeled herself for the confrontation to come. She had told herself, many times as she'd tossed and turned the night before, that things would look better in the daylight. However, imagined conversations rarely went the way you had rehearsed them in real life.

As she locked the car door out of habit, she heard footsteps behind her and turned to see the last person she had wanted to meet first. She forced a smile. "Hello, Robin."

"Well, well. The famous Professor Moss." Robin gave her a sarcastic grin. "Guess you've come to grovel, again."

"I'm here to see Den, if that's what you mean." She kept her tone level, determined not to let Robin's overt aggressiveness put her off balance.

"She's in the living room."

Kathryn felt Robin's eyes boring into her back as she entered the house. Denise was sitting on the floor, back against the sofa, reading. One of the cats, the smaller of the two, lay stretched out next to her and Den's hand was idly stroking it. She stood watching her, not wanting to disturb the peaceful scene. The tightness in her chest ratcheted up a notch.

The cat noticed her first, swivelling its head towards her. Alerted by the animal's movement, Den looked up and saw her silhouetted against the open doorway. She didn't move but the cat made a show of stretching itself and walking off to find another comfortable perch.

Kathryn stepped into the room and closed the door. "Den. Look, about last night. I'm sorry, I hadn't expected to see you there."

Den drew her knees up to her chest and hugged them. She looked away from Kathryn. She said quietly, "Maybe if you'd bothered to ring me back you would have known. At the very least you could have told me not to bother coming up."

The conversation had already hit a brick wall. Kathryn sat down on the edge of the armchair with the space of the wooden coffee table between them.

"I didn't want to give you this news over the phone. I was planning to come down to London next week."

"What news?" Den asked, the dullness of her tone indicating she knew what was coming.

"I've accepted the Durham job. I'm sorry. It's nothing personal. The job, the location, it's all a better fit for what I want to do."

"Well, that's great. Just great." Den still wasn't looking at her.

"Den, please. This isn't easy for me. I do care about you."

"Do you?" Den asked with tears streaming down her face.

Kathryn was astonished to see the pain in Den's eyes.

"But it's not enough, is it? You don't love me."

Kathryn put her head in her hands. Of all the words that had passed through her mind during the night, this wasn't one she had expected to encounter. Love. What did she know about love? She had no experience of long-term relationships. Six months was usually her limit. And the only woman who had crossed that line was Ellie Winters, and she was unavailable now.

When she first met Den she didn't think she was the settling down kind either. Now Den was showing signs of wanting commitment and she really couldn't give her that. And right now, after the week she'd had, she really couldn't handle this display of emotional turmoil either.

†

Ellie was putting her brushes away. When they'd returned from Hebden, she told Robin and Den she needed to get back to her current work in progress and had gone straight into her studio. Now, though, the afternoon light was moving to the far side of the building so she knew it was time to stop for the day.

Robin appeared in the doorway just as she finished cleaning up. Her T-shirt was smeared with a dark substance that also had found its way onto her cheeks. She looked like an extra for *Grease*. Ellie smiled at her. It was only Robin's mechanical know-how that was keeping their ancient Jeep running and she had said she was going to tune it up after the drive back.

The Jeep had been her father's last purchase before he died and it had meant so much to him Ellie couldn't bear to part with it. She wasn't sure how much longer it would be roadworthy with parts getting harder to find. Robin seemed to enjoy the challenge though.

"Hey, don't you look good enough to eat," Ellie teased, moving in for a kiss.

"Yeah. As long as you don't mind the taste of petrol."

"Blends in with the turps, I'd say." Ellie gripped her belt loops and pulled her closer. Robin bent her head for the kiss. She broke off before Ellie was ready, a look tinged with concern in her normally clear hazel eyes.

"The Professor's here."

"Oh." Ellie moved a hand round and gave her lover's lean butt a possessive squeeze. "I don't know why you're worried about her, hon. There is nothing left between us."

"Maybe not for you." Robin ran her tongue around her lips. "Why do you think she's playing hard to get with Den?"

"Kathryn's not the marrying kind. Her career will always come first. I tried to explain that to Den last night, but I don't think she was listening."

"Do you think it will disturb them if we go through to the kitchen? I could murder a beer."

"We'll creep in quietly," Ellie said, taking her hand.

†

The scene that met their eyes when they arrived in the house wasn't what they expected. Neither of the other two women was speaking. Kathryn was sitting on the couch, head in her hands, staring at the floor. Den was just getting to her feet from a near foetal position, uncurling her long legs with difficulty.

Ellie was shocked to see that her face was streaked with tears.

Den looked over at them. "Oh good. Rob, do you think you could take me to the train station? I can be ready to go in a few minutes."

"Den, you don't have to leave now. Even if you get a good connection you won't be back in London until near midnight."

"I don't care. I have to go."

Kathryn looked up then. "Please, Den. We need to talk about this."

Den ignored her and covered the distance to the stairs in a few strides.

Robin let go of Ellie's hand. "I'm going to get a drink. Do you want anything, love?"

"No, thanks." Ellie watched her partner disappear into the kitchen and turned to the professor. "What are you playing at, Kathryn? Don't you have any feelings for Den?"

"Of course I do."

"So, what's going on? She's obviously very upset."

"She wanted me to take the London job, but it's not for me."

"So, you're going to Durham?"

"Yes." Kathryn stood up and walked towards her.

Ellie watched her warily. It seemed Robin was right; Kathryn hadn't completely let go. She held up her hand to stop her former lover from getting too close. Inconsequentially, she noticed a streak of red paint running down her thumb. "Kathryn. I thought we'd got past this."

"You might have, Ellie. But she never has." Den was standing at the bottom of the stairs with her rucksack. "That's her problem. She's still wrapped up in the romance, finding the bones of Queen Cartimandua and her female lover."

"Den!" Kathryn's voice held a warning tone.

"Oh, sorry. That was a secret, wasn't it? Never trust a journalist. That's what you really think of me, isn't it? Well, fuck you! Have a nice life." She turned to Ellie. "I'll wait outside for Robin. Thanks for everything."

Ellie watched her stalk out in stunned silence. "Is that true?" she whispered.

Kathryn was still staring at the door. She turned back to Ellie. "Yes. I've managed to keep it out of the media so far. I didn't want you to go through what you did last summer. It will become public knowledge once the exhibition opens, though."

"I think you could have told me."

Kathryn held up her hands. "It's not like she's still buried here. People won't be trekking out here to put pens or poems on her grave like they do for Sylvia Plath over at Heptonstall."

"It could become a lesbian pilgrimage, though. A site of herstorical interest."

"I can't really see that happening." Kathryn reached out to touch her.

Ellie pushed her hand away. "You're unbelievable. Don't you think you should go out and try to talk to Den?"

"Why? She hates me now."

"You don't have a clue, do you? She's in love with you, Kathryn. And right now she's hurting. If you have any feelings for her at all, you'll go outside now and talk to her."

"I don't know what to say."

"Sorry, might be a start."

"The Professor doesn't do 'sorry'." Robin came into the room, one hand wrapped around a cold bottle of Corona. She had, Ellie noticed, washed her hands but only managed to smudge the marks on her face. With her hair sticking up in places she had the look of an undernourished street urchin.

Ellie moved over to her lover and wrapped an arm around her slim waist. "Better not have too much beer, sweets. It looks like you'll need to take Den to the station."

Kathryn gave the pair a long look, then turned on her heel. "I'll talk to her," she said as she went out.

Part Two

Chapter Four

Works in Progress

Robin waited on the platform with the still distraught journalist. Even with taking a few risks on the bike and exceeding the speed limit for most of the journey from the farm, Den had missed a train to Leeds by a few minutes. But it was only a ten-minute wait for the next one. Friday evening and the platform filled up quickly with more passengers.

"You might not get a seat on the London train," Robin said.

"Doesn't matter." Den stared down the track.

"Do you want a coffee?"

"No, thanks."

Robin left her and went over to the platform kiosk. She returned a few minutes later and handed Den a paper bag.

"What's this?"

"Going away present. You probably won't get near the buffet car either, so take it."

Den looked inside the bag. Nestled next to a well-filled tuna and sweet corn sandwich were two cans of lager.

"Sorry, there wasn't a great choice of beer."

Den smiled for the first time since their lunch in Hebden Bridge. "Thanks, mate."

"Hey, Ellie wouldn't forgive me if I didn't give you some sustenance. Believe me, if there had been time, she would have sent you off with a three-course meal."

Den looked close to tears again.

Robin glanced at the announcement board. Five minutes to the arrival of the next train. Hard to believe it was less than twenty-four hours since she had first spotted Den at the Town Hall. And Den looked even worse, if that was possible, than she had on that occasion.

"Look, Den, I know this is a pile of shite, but…"

"If you tell me, 'this too will pass,' I'll deck you."

"Okay. I won't say that. But just remember you have friends. We're here for you."

"Thanks."

"And you'll let us know, won't you, if you decide to run off and join the Moonies or something?"

"Yeah." She almost managed another smile.

There was a surge towards the edge of the platform; the train was approaching. Robin gave Den a quick hug and watched her get on the train. She sensibly pressed herself into a corner by the far door. Years of travelling on public transport in London, Robin thought the journalist would cope with the cramped fifteen-minute journey to Leeds. But she didn't envy her the two and a half hours on the crowded train headed south on a warm summer's evening.

She returned to her bike and set off back home.

†

When Robin handed her the bag on the platform at Huddersfield, Den didn't think she would eat the sandwich. The beer she was grateful for, but the idea of eating made her feel ill. However, by the time the train passed Doncaster, she was ready for it and she had managed to grab a seat, so although the train was crowded, she was reasonably comfortable. Restful for her body, but not her mind.

Kathryn had come out of the farmhouse and they had stared at each other, like a couple of gunslingers in a Western movie. Just when she thought Kathryn was going to say something, the professor simply shook her head, turned away and got into her car. Den watched in stunned disbelief as she drove off. Ellie came outside just as the red car disappeared from view.

"Did she say anything to you?" Ellie asked, concern showing in her blue eyes.

Den couldn't speak. She was on the verge of breaking down again. Ellie pulled her into a hug and she wept on the smaller woman's shoulder. Robin came out and waited while she recovered herself and Ellie released her. Then she silently handed her a helmet and went over to the motorbike. Den thanked Ellie again and mounted the bike behind Robin. The breakneck speed of the journey to the train station gave her something else to worry about but she only just managed to hold herself together while waiting on the platform.

Arriving home at this late hour, her plan was to slip into the house quietly and hope everyone else was in bed. Approaching the end of the street, she was surprised to see all the lights on and as she got nearer she could hear music as well. A party. *Great. Just what she didn't need.* Henry hadn't mentioned a party but he thought she was staying up north for the weekend.

The blast of music hit her when she opened the front door, mingled with the noise of people talking loudly to make themselves heard. The recognisable smell of marijuana assaulted her nostrils at the same time. She didn't usually indulge in smoking weed but she wouldn't have minded a few good hits from a generously rolled joint right now. She started up the stairs, just wanting to reach the sanctuary of her room. The bathroom door opened as she was brushing discreetly past two men in a close embrace in the hallway and she came face-to-face with Henry.

"Hey, what're you doing here?" He reached out to her. She pushed past him and took the stairs two at a time up to her eyrie. Henry followed. She wasn't quick enough and he barged into the room before she could close the door on him.

"What happened? I thought you were good up there."

Den dumped her bag on the floor by the bed and turned to face him. "Nothing happened. That's what. She doesn't want me." She couldn't stop the tears from leaking out. The emotion she'd been holding in since leaving Huddersfield flowed out.

Henry didn't hesitate. He embraced her and waited patiently while she cried. He released her when she'd calmed down and sat next to her on the bed, handing her tissues.

"Where did you stay last night? I thought you were with her."

Den gave him the details knowing he wouldn't leave her alone until she talked.

"I don't understand. I don't know what went wrong. It wasn't like I wanted us to get married or anything. I just wanted to spend more time with her."

"And you think she's still in love with this Ellie?"

"Yes. Fuck. It's like some bad soap opera. What am I going to do, Hen?"

He gripped her knee firmly. "Well, I've never understood dyke relationships. And, I have to say, I'm as baffled as you are. I thought she was really nice. I even slipped a piece of my homemade apple pie into her briefcase before she left."

Den snorted. "Right. What kind of woman could resist that?"

They sat in silence for a few minutes.

"Is it a special occasion?" she asked finally.

"What?"

"This party. It's not your usual civilised soirée."

"Paul's ex. It's his birthday."

Den gave him a half-hearted grin. "And you don't understand dyke relationships? You guys are just as bad."

He ignored her comment. "Look. I know you're hurting right now. But give it time. She might just be sorting things out. New job, moving house, all that."

"She didn't have to just shut me out, though. If she thought she could get Ellie Winters into bed, she wouldn't be thinking about any of that."

"So, what's she like, this femme fatale of the north?"

"Ellie's lovely. I mean I can totally understand the attraction. But she and Robin, well you'd need a chisel to pry them apart. They're very different, but they just belong together, if you know what I mean."

He nodded. "Yeah. I get that. Listen, this party will be going on for a while, do you want to come down for a drink?"

"Thanks, but I'll pass."

"Okay. I'll bring something up. I bet you haven't eaten at all."

"I had a tuna sandwich on the train."

"I think I can do better than that."

He was as good as his word, as usual. Ten minutes later he returned with a tray laden with an elaborate cheese plate, including grapes and celery, and a chilled bottle of Sancerre.

"Looking after my health, I see," Den said as she picked up a celery stick.

He poured her a generous measure of wine. "I'll leave you the bottle. Eat, drink, and pass out. See you tomorrow."

"It's already tomorrow," she said to his back as he departed, closing the door softly.

Lying awake in the dark room, not drunk enough to pass out as Henry had suggested, she wondered again what had happened. Two weeks ago, in this very bed, Kathryn had seemed happy to be with her. They had made love on and off for hours. She would have known, wouldn't she, if Kathryn had been faking it? Just remembering the intensity of their passion, her clit started to throb.

She reached between her legs and began to stroke herself, amazed at how wet she was. Closing her eyes she could see Kathryn's breasts hovering above her just tantalisingly out of reach of her mouth. Arching upwards she was able to capture an erect nipple in her mouth. Her hand gained momentum as she inserted two fingers inside her aching core. Within minutes she came with a loud moan, crying out Kathryn's name.

She wiped her hand on the sheet and rolled over. There was no way Kathryn could have been pretending to enjoy making love with her. The professor was a demanding lover and gave as good as she got. Was she thinking of Ellie the whole time? No, she wouldn't dwell on that. It was madness to even think that way. And it wasn't even as if she had the satisfaction of hating the other woman. Ellie had only ever treated her with kindness.

Giving up on the idea of sleep, Den turned the bedside lamp on and reached for her laptop. Might as well try and catch up on some reading. She logged into her news aggregator, Flipboard, and checked the day's feeds. Nothing could quite grab her attention for any length of time. For something lighter, she checked the Huffington Post site. Finally, after sifting through her friend posts on Facebook and her Twitter timeline, she found she was no nearer sleep mode.

The party was still going strong—she could hear strains of songs she didn't recognise. Must be getting old. The bottle of wine was almost empty. She finished it off and lay down again. This time sleep came quickly.

†

Kathryn paced around her living room, the book-lined walls, usually a source of comfort, felt like they were closing in on her. There was no getting away from the fact that she knew she had acted badly. The look on Den's face as she drove away from the farm was haunting her. Could she really let it end like this? She did care about Den. Her friendship was important to her. But it was no use having a full complement of academic degrees if you couldn't behave like a decent human being. The worst of it was that it was Ellie's obvious disappointment in her that bothered her most.

Checking her watch again—it was after midnight and too late to call anyone. Her plans for the next day included driving to Lytham St Anne's to see her parents. She'd last seen them at Christmas and owed them a visit. At this rate she would arrive looking like hell and have to put up with her mother fussing about her not looking after herself and asking why couldn't she find a nice man to settle down with?

Kathryn considered asking Ed to come along to give her cover but he would be bored out of his mind when left to talk to her father, who would want to educate him on the finer points of golf. She played a bit herself but rarely found time these days to fit in a round. Her parents were both mad keen and had sold the family home in Sheffield twenty years ago to retire to the seaside and play golf every day. She did need to fit this visit in before the start of The Open Championship, which was taking place not far from them at Hoylake. They would be there for the full four days. At seventy-seven and seventy-eight neither showed signs of slowing down and she was grateful they were both fit and healthy and enjoying life when so many their age were either in nursing homes or in the grave.

†

The drive to the coast was peaceful early on a Saturday. A bright summer morning and she hoped to beat the families heading out for a day by the seaside. Before setting off, Kathryn plugged her iPod into the car's music system and let the gentle country style of Nanci Griffith soothe her troubled thoughts. Arriving at her parents' smart bungalow, she parked on the road. It was likely that one or both of them would be taking their car out to go to the golf course some-time during that morning.

Her mother opened the door as she approached.

"You're early, dear."

"No traffic." Kathryn pecked her on the cheek and fol-lowed her inside.

"No matter. Dad's making pancakes."

Greeting her father with a hug, she sat down at the kitch-en table, feeling about twelve years old again as her parents carried on with their breakfast preparations around her. Mum poured coffee and set the table while her dad prepared the pancakes, making her smile as he showed off by flipping them deftly. She knew it was no use offering to help.

It wasn't difficult to keep up a conversation. After they had updated her on their golf handicaps—going up or down another point one after the last competition—she told them about her decision to go to Durham. They had both been teachers in grammar schools and recognised the significance of the move for her—a step up in her career.

After breakfast her mother disappeared to get dressed for golf. "Mixed doubles match, summer knockout comp," she explained as she collected her shoes from the cupboard by the front door. Her clubs and electric trolley were already in the car. "See you later," she called as she breezed out.

Kathryn helped her father clean up the breakfast dishes and then he suggested a walk along the beach. The tide was a long way out and she slipped off her sandals, enjoying the softness of the sand between her toes. After a time, they found a place to sit.

"So, do you want to talk about it?" he asked.

"About what?"

"About whatever is bothering you. And don't tell me you're worried about the new job or having to move house. It's deeper than that. I can see it in your eyes."

"Am I that transparent?" Kathryn kept her eyes on the skyline.

"Well, you turn up at the crack of dawn looking like you haven't slept in a week. Doesn't take a genius to work out that something's up and it's not work or money. I guess it must be a woman."

"Dad!"

"Oh, it's all right. We know. I mean we've always suspected. But Phil let slip about someone you were seeing last time he was here."

Phil, her younger brother. Of course. He'd met Den not so long ago. One of her visits to London when they had gone to the theatre and ran into him purely by chance. She could hardly say Den was just a colleague when they had their arms wrapped around each other. She hadn't expected him to go blabbing to her parents. He never could keep a secret, though.

"It's complicated and I'm not sure I want to talk about it."

"Sometimes it helps. It doesn't do any good to keep things bottled up."

"I think I've screwed it up, so it doesn't matter."

He took her hand and gently massaged her knuckles. "It matters to me, Katya. I want you to be happy."

She felt tears start at his use of her childhood nickname. It took her some time but he waited patiently and didn't interrupt when she started to talk. She told him about meeting Ellie Winters and how she had let that relationship lapse. Then the dig at Ellie's farm had stirred up her feelings for her again. But Ellie was in love with someone else and had now married her. She explained about meeting Den and being attracted to her. And now Den wanted some kind of commitment and she'd pushed her away.

"Okay. So Den thinks you're still in love with Ellie. Are you?"

"I guess. I don't know. I'm confused."

He took both her hands in his and looked at her. "This isn't like my rational, logical, intelligent daughter." He broke his gaze and stared out to sea. The tide had turned but it would be another hour before the water reached them. "Seems to me you have to forget Ellie. From what you say, her love lies elsewhere. So, the question is are you really interested in Den, or has the relationship run its course?"

"I don't know. I like being with Den. We always have fun together."

"But that isn't enough for her?"

"No. She made that clear."

"Well, you're starting a new job. So, a fresh start. If you don't think a long-distance relationship is viable with her, and it doesn't sound like it is, then now's the perfect time to make the break."

Kathryn sighed and stood up. She gazed at the encroaching water. "Time to go back, Dad." She gave him a bleak smile. "But thanks for the pep talk."

He stood and hugged her. His enveloping smell of sea air, pancake mix, and aftershave surrounded her and she felt herself relax against him. When he let go, she put her sandals on and they walked back to the house discussing the chances of various well-known professional golfers winning the Open. The one thing they both agreed on was the hope for some wet and windy weather to make it an interesting contest instead of the standard blast it down the fairway, then pitch and putt.

†

Jasmine couldn't think over the roaring in her head. Sex with Robin had been great, but this experience was beyond words. Slowly, as her breathing calmed, rational thought returned. She licked her lips and opened her eyes. A hand slick with her juices reached around to touch her lips. She licked the fingers, tasting herself and starting to feel aroused again. Lying facedown on the bed, hands and feet handcuffed to the frame she wanted nothing more than to stay in here forever, anticipating more pleasure.

Max's low-pitched voice floated above her. "I know you want more. But it will have to wait."

Jasmine moaned softly as the cuffs were unlocked one by one.

"Don't move." Max's voice was firm. "Count to one hundred, then get dressed and leave by the front door. There will be a taxi waiting to take you home. I'll call you."

Jasmine heard her leave the room. She started counting.

Moving slowly, she gingerly flexed her hands and waited for the numbness to subside. Her feet felt okay. She eased herself sideways off the bed and stood. It took a few more deep breaths before she felt steady enough to look for her clothes. They were neatly folded on the chair by the window.

The room had an en-suite bathroom and she desperately needed to pee.

Later, at home, relaxing in a bath, she tried to make sense of the last few hours. The euphoria hadn't worn off. Where had she been? It was like visiting another country and not knowing the language. But she was completely at ease with it. Ever since the night at the leather club—*was it really only a week ago?*—she had been in a heightened state of sexual desire. Just the thought of Max's touch had her insides fluttering.

Sleep didn't come easily. She drifted in and out of consciousness, disappointed when awareness returned, that she wasn't still tied to Max's bed.

The next morning Jas thought about going to the gym or trying a short jog but these thoughts passed easily through her head. The thought of a Starbucks coffee was more enticing. *Bugger the calories, she was going to have a full fat, large cappuccino.* She felt virtuous sprinkling the froth with nutmeg instead of chocolate. Her phone lay silent on the table in front of her. She had set a special ringtone for Max and she didn't want to miss her call.

She was just scraping the remnants of froth from the bottom of the cup when the phone buzzed. It was a text from Den. *Call me.* She looked at it guiltily. Her last conversation with her friend had been brief and she knew she shouldn't have cut her off.

"Hey, where are you?" Den didn't even wait for her to say hello.

"Starbucks, Highbury."

"Figures. I'm at Oxford Street. If the tube's running to time I can be with you in fifteen. You okay to stay there?"

"Yeah. What's up?" But Den had already disconnected.

Jasmine moved to the recently vacated comfortable seats by the window and flicked through the newspaper left on the table. After ten minutes she ordered a flat latte for herself and a cappuccino for Den. The coffees were ready just as Den walked through the door. One glance at her face and Jas could see she wasn't in a good state of mind.

Den caught her look and said, "You don't need to say it. I look like shit."

"So, what's happened? Last time we met you were looking forward to a shag-fest with the professor."

"It didn't quite go as planned." Den ran her fingers through her hair and sighed. "I mean we did end up having a great weekend together. Then, well, I don't know. It's like a switch flicked off. She went back up north and I heard nothing from her. One measly text to say she was on the train. Then Henry found out she was doing a talk at Huddersfield Town Hall. He booked me a train ticket and everything. I thought maybe I could talk to her. But she blanked me."

Jas looked at her, concerned. Den was close to tears.

"She didn't speak to you at all?"

"Well, sort of. I met Robin after the talk and she took me back to Starling Hill. I mean I hadn't booked any accommodation. I thought I would be staying with her. She turned up at the farm the next day. Maybe she meant to apologise, but it didn't feel like it. And when Ellie appeared, it was all she could do to keep her hands off her. I mean, fuck it, Jas. Can't she see that Ellie's wrapped up with Robin? Can't she let go?"

Jas could hear the anguish in Den's voice. She reached across the table and grasped her hand. "I'm so sorry. I haven't been much use to you, either."

Den sipped her coffee. "No. So, what's going on? I feel like crap, but you're practically glowing."

"Hard to explain." Jas let go of her hand and picked up her own drink.

"Come on. This is me you're talking to. Max Fleetwood. From what Steph said, she's pretty heavy-duty."

"Depends on your point of view."

"So, you've gone over to the dark side after just a few dates."

Jas laughed. "If this is the dark side, I'm all for it. I've never felt so…fulfilled."

"Yeah, well, if it all goes pear-shaped, give me a call and I'll sort her out."

"You're so butch."

"Leave it out. You're my mate."

"I wish I could help you out with what's-her-name."

"Thanks, but I think it's over now. I just have to get her out of my system. Maybe I should try this leather scene."

Jas smiled at her fondly. "You wouldn't last five minutes before you decked someone."

They finished their coffees and headed out onto the street. Jas promised to meet up again soon. She waved good-bye to her on the corner and checked her phone once more, willing it to ring.

†

Talking to Jas had helped ease the pain in her chest, but as Den walked through the busy streets, crowded with Saturday shoppers and tourists, images of Kathryn came back to her. Getting the professor out of her system wasn't going to be easy. Den wandered aimlessly, barely conscious of the people around her. Eventually, aware that she was still in the environs of North London, she found her way to King's Cross and took the Piccadilly line to Hyde Park Corner.

Walking through the park always helped to calm her thoughts. When she was working on a story, trying to fit pieces together, she would make the journey to the large parkland in the middle of the city either by bus or tube. Sitting under one of the ancient trees she could watch passersby and put things in perspective. Today she found herself drawn to the Serpentine and parked herself on the grass by the large man-made lake—an ideal spot to sit and observe.

A whiff of cigarette smoke from a couple strolling past and she wanted to stop them to cadge a cig. She had never been a serious smoker. Like a former US President, she had never mastered the art of inhaling. It was more of a prop. At school she'd smoked to fit in with the cool kids. Later on, at work, it was a way to take a break. And the time spent in bars, chasing leads, it seemed to go with the drinking culture. When the smoking ban came into force, she just stopped one day and it was only at times like this, stressed out, when she thought she really wanted to light one up. Usually one puff was enough, though, to remind her that she didn't really like the taste or the burn in her throat.

A sunny day, sitting in London's greatest green space, watching the world pass by. What could be better? Kathryn was two hundred miles away and wouldn't be thinking about her. 'Don't worry about things you can't change,' her mother had always advised her at various times as she lurched through her tumultuous teenage years. She had been the problem child, not knowing what she wanted. Starting projects and not finishing them. Her parents had been disappointed she hadn't completed her master's degree in English literature. She had been living at home until she was twenty-five paying off her university fees. Henry's offer of a room when he bought the house in Chiswick had been a lifesaver. Finally out of the family home, she had started to make her own way. Still, what did she have to show for twenty years? She didn't own a car, have a mortgage, and now, it seemed she couldn't even manage to sustain a relationship.

Her phone vibrated in her pocket. Den pulled it out, heart hammering. Could it be Kathryn calling?

No. The phone showed her editor's face. *Fuck!* She hadn't forgotten a deadline, had she?

"Hey, Tom." She opted for a casual tone.

"Hey yourself. Listen, got some more old bones for you to check out. Could be bigger than that Starling Hill gig."

"Where?"

"Some shithole near Bournemouth."

"If it's near Bournemouth, it won't be a shithole."

"Whatever. Just haul your ass down there and poke around."

Den grinned to herself. Tom liked to talk like an extra in a spaghetti Western.

"So, do I get any more info? Other than near Bournemouth?"

"Already winging its way, smart dude. I'll expect the dope on this by Weds latest. And I expect it to be the dogs' bollocks."

"One word. Expenses."

"Don't sweat it, Sullivan. Pick up a staff car. Shithole's in the middle of fucking nowhere. Chow." He was gone.

She sat for a few more minutes, and then opened the email when it pinged on her phone. Looked like an interesting assignment. Den read through it a second time. Well, at least it was far enough away from Yorkshire. She wasn't likely to meet any archaeologists she knew in Winterborne Kingston.

The car was a battered Ford Fiesta, only a few years old, but it had suffered at the hands of any number of extremely careless journos. Den took it to the nearest garage, filled a plastic bag with empty cans and wrappers and used the vac to make it acceptable for the long journey ahead. She wasn't a neat freak herself but she objected to sitting in someone else's tip.

When she arrived back home it was nearing three o'clock, and she wanted to hit the road soon to be sure of finding somewhere to stay before it got dark. She dashed up to her room to pack the essentials. Henry emerged from the kitchen as she reached the bottom of the stairs with her rucksack and laptop bag.

"Where to?" he asked, wiping his hands on his apron.

"Somewhere near Bournemouth."

"Right. Spur of the moment hol? Visit with your folks. Good idea."

"No. It's work. Maybe some Roman skeletons."

"Okay." He hugged her. "Keep in touch."

"Sure, Mum."

"Hey, wait, don't move." He dashed back into the kitchen.

She waited at the door. He returned a few minutes later with a carrier bag. "Supplies. Water and some nibbles."

"Thanks, Hen. If you weren't already spoken for, I'd marry you."

"Get off, you big dyke." He kissed her cheek affectionately. "Drive carefully."

†

Checking the map Den turned off the M3 to head for a place called Blandford Forum that looked to be the biggest settlement of any size near the dig site. As she slowed down to drive through the delightfully named village of Pimperne, a few miles short of Blandford Forum, she spotted a small inn with a thatched roof.

The drive had taken a little over two hours and this seemed as good a place as any to grab a bite to eat. She decided to stop and if she liked the look of it she would see if they had any rooms available. *Fuck the cost. It was on expenses.* Although, another half hour's drive and she could be at her parents' house in Poole. However, the thought passed quickly through her mind, as she couldn't face telling them about another failure in her life.

✝

The house was quiet. Henry enjoyed the weekends he was able to spend at home. What he called family time with Paul. He thought that if they had hooked up sooner, it would have been great to have kids. But for a long time he hadn't been interested in settling down.

Paul arrived back from the shop with the Sunday paper. They spread out on the living room floor, enjoying the peace of the day together, Paul with the sports section, he with the main news. The doorbell chimed when he was only on page five.

Paul looked up. "It's still early. You expecting anyone, Hen?"

"No. Might be Steph if she's forgotten her key." He scrambled to his feet and went out into the hallway.

The visitor standing nervously on the doorstep was possibly the last person he would have expected to see early on a Sunday morning.

"Dr Moss," he said flatly.

"Um, hi. Sorry to disturb you. Is Den in?"

"No, she's not."

"Look, I know you probably don't think much of me, but I really need to talk to her."

"Have you tried phoning her?"

"Yes, but she's not answering."

"Then I guess she doesn't want to talk to you."

"Henry. I know I've screwed this up. But I would like the chance to make it right, if I can."

He softened his stance. The woman looked worn-out. She was dressed casually in cargo shorts and a loose-fitting

T-shirt, canvas slip-ons on her feet. Her hair, which he'd re-called as being stylishly cut, was in disarray, loose strands brushing across her face. Despite the worry lines though, he would have put her a good ten years younger than what he knew her age to be.

"She really isn't here. Why don't you come in and have a coffee?"

"Okay, thanks."

Henry led the way down the short hallway to the kitchen. He put the kettle on.

"Would you like something to eat?"

"Maybe some toast, if that's not too much trouble."

Henry made coffee and toast and sat down at the table opposite her. Paul had poked his head in to see who their guest was, but Henry shook his head at him and he returned to the living room.

"Have you come down by train?"

"No. I drove. I was at my parents' place yesterday. That's at Lytham. Anyway the M6 was clear for most of the way and at least you're on the western edge of the city here."

He regarded her silently. It wasn't really his business to meddle but Den was a dear friend and seeing the pain she was in Friday night had hurt. All because this woman couldn't make her mind up. But she had driven a few hundred miles this morning to see Den.

Kathryn finished her toast and looked up at him. "She told you what happened, or rather, what didn't happen, I guess."

"Yes." He hesitated. "Den and I go back a long way. She's family as far as I'm concerned. I don't want to see her suffering like this."

"I'm struggling a bit here, Henry. This is uncharted terri-tory for me and I've obviously not handled it very well. Is Den coming back here today?"

"Not for a few days. She's on an assignment near Bournemouth."

"What kind of assignment?"

"I don't really know. She just said something about some bones being discovered."

"You don't know where in Bournemouth?"

"No, that's all she said. I only saw her briefly as she was leaving yesterday."

Kathryn swallowed the last of her coffee. "Thanks for your hospitality, once again. I know I'm not particularly welcome, but I appreciate it."

"You look done in. Do you want to crash here for a few hours?"

"Thanks for the offer. But I think I'd best be on my way now."

"I'm not sure you should. Believe me, I have experience with long-haul flights. I don't think you should be driving anywhere until you've had a rest." He watched her closely, her eyelids were drooping again. "Come on. Upstairs. Before you fall asleep at the table."

†

Kathryn came to in a strange room. Her body and limbs felt heavy. Still drowsy, she looked around cautiously. Light was coming through the long windows at the far end. Slowly regaining consciousness she realised she was in Den's room. Her overnight bag was by the bed. She vaguely remembered Henry asking for her keys before she passed out. Something about having to move the car.

It felt unreal. She was in Den's room; she could smell her scent on the pillow and the memories of their passionate lovemaking flooded through her. Was it really only two weeks ago? She groped around for her glasses and putting

88

them on glanced at her watch. It was three thirty. Unbelievable. She'd slept for six hours.

Moving slowly, she sat up. There was a large bath towel on the chair near the bed with a note on it. She stood up and went over to read it. *Bathroom is at the bottom of the stairs, hair dryer in cupboard.* Henry certainly knew how to look after a woman's needs. Did she smell bad from the long drive or had her hair turned into a rat's nest? When she saw her reflection in the mirror in the bathroom she decided it was definitely the hair.

Half an hour later, feeling refreshed and more alive than she had for a few days, she sat down at Den's desk under the window and opened up her laptop. It still had the Wi-Fi password from her previous visit so she was able to access her emails. Nothing of any importance there. She scrolled through her contacts list and found the one she was looking for, the archaeologist she had talked to at a conference the previous year, and now a professor at Bournemouth University. Wording the email to him carefully, she mentioned that she was in the area and would he mind if she came along to look at the skeletons he had recently unearthed. It was a fishing expedition and nothing might come of it, but it was worth a try. Dorset was home to the Jurassic Coast and there were numerous sites still needing excavation, not just for the discovery of fossils, but Roman remains as well. As in modern times, it had been a popular area for wealthy citizens to settle.

†

Wondering if her hosts were still in the house, she ventured down the stairs and found her way to the kitchen. The patio doors were open so she went outside. It was a lovely warm afternoon and the enclosed garden was bathed in sunlight. Paul was kneeling by a flowerbed, weeding.

"Hi," she said.

He looked up at her and smiled. "Hi. You're looking better."

"Thanks. Did I really look so wrecked earlier?"

"Yeah, you did. Henry was quite worried about you."

"Well, I can't thank him enough. It seems I really needed the sleep. And the shower."

He stood up and brushed his knees off. "I'm ready for a cuppa. Would you like one?"

"Yes, thanks. Can I do anything?"

"No, just take a seat. I won't be long."

She sat on one of the deck chairs and breathed in the air. It wasn't as fresh as the air she was used to in the north, but the flowering shrubs in the garden gave it a pleasing aroma. The house was close to the Thames she remembered. And when the tide was out, it gave off a pungent odour. Den hadn't seemed to be aware of it when they had walked along by the river before, but it had made her want to just take shallow breaths.

Paul came out with a tray and placed it on the wicker table between the chairs. "I'll be mother," he said as he sat down. "Milk?" he asked, holding up the tiny jug. Kathryn nodded and watched as he carefully put a small amount in each cup. He poured the tea into the beautiful china cups with matching saucers and handed her one. "Sugar?"

"No thanks."

They sat quietly, sipping their tea. She accepted a biscuit as well. One of her favourite kinds, ginger. *No wonder Den likes living here.*

"You're not working today?" She knew from her last visit that he was a nurse and worked shifts so it wasn't unknown for him to be working on a weekend.

"No. It's great my timetable meshed with Henry's for a change. I'm back on the wards Monday night and he's setting off that evening for Australia."

"It must be hard, if he's away so much."

"Sometimes. But if Den or Steph are around I have some company. Anyway, it works for us."

"Where's Henry now?"

"Went out for a jog, should be back any minute."

"Don't you jog?"

"Not anymore. My knees can't take it. I work out at the gym instead."

As if on cue, they heard the front door opening. Henry arrived in the garden seconds later, wiping sweat from his brow. "Hey, Sleeping Beauty's up!"

"Yes, I really conked out." She smiled at him. "Look, I don't know how to thank you. Can I take you both out to dinner?"

"As it happens, we're booked at The Dove. Their menu is a cut above most pub fare and we have a table on the terrace overlooking the river for this evening. I'm sure they could squeeze you in."

"Sounds wonderful."

†

Later, as they sat on the terrace watching the summer evening activity on the river, rowers and small pleasure boats, Kathryn felt a twinge of guilt. She had received an answer from her Bournemouth contact. He was excited about the finds at Winterborne Kingston and would be delighted to show her around, inviting her to visit the site the next day. She had immediately emailed back to say she would be there by late morning. This was information she hadn't shared with Henry and Paul. They thought she was heading back up north.

Before going to bed, she looked up the site location and found a roadside inn only a few miles away that looked like it had suitable accommodation. The deciding factor was the free Wi-Fi, so she made a reservation for two nights.

Sitting at Den's desk, she watched the darkening sky, the lights shining from houses across the street. A different kind of view, she found she missed the open spaces, the hills. Finding paper in the printer she took out two blank sheets. Was there some way she could tell Den what was important to her, without making it sound like she was making excuses? She scribbled a note, crossed half of it out and started again. Writing a ten thousand word essay with references would be easier. It took several drafts before she was satisfied. Even then she wasn't sure she had expressed herself very well.

Next morning, having once again slept soundly, she enjoyed another of Henry's delightful breakfasts before taking her leave of the two men, thanking them profusely. They parted amicably, Henry even offering to phone Den for her. He said she would answer if the call was from his phone. Kathryn declined, saying she didn't want to disturb her as she was working. She just asked that they let Den know she had been there when she returned home and that she wanted to talk to her.

The Monday rush hour traffic was heavier heading into London so she was pleased to be heading out...to The West...as the sign said. And once she left the M3 for the A354 she enjoyed the drive through the countryside. She stopped just outside Salisbury to have a coffee and stretch her legs. It was another fine day and she thought that whatever happened with Den, she was at least going to enjoy being on the site of an archaeological dig.

†

The weekend had passed in slow motion for Jasmine. She could only hang on to her memories of Friday night and Saturday morning, replaying them in an endless loop, to keep herself sane. Max didn't phone. Was this all part of the game? If so, she wasn't familiar with the rules. The only rule she instinctively knew was that she had to wait. Max was in control. She would call when she wanted her and when the call came Jas would drop whatever she was doing and go to her.

Den hadn't called either. A brief text said she was going out of town on an assignment. Well, at least she had a distraction. Jas was reduced to watching Wimbledon doubles matches and flicking through the channels to find something that would take her mind off her awakened libido. She had never masturbated so much in her life. She was wet with desire just thinking about what Max had in store for her.

When her mother phoned Saturday evening she caught her off guard, asking if there was anyone special in her life. Her mother seemed to have an uncanny knack of knowing when something was happening with her. Perhaps it was because she was an only child. Surprised she had just said, yes. When her mother pressed for more information she admitted she was seeing someone called Max and, without thinking, added the details that Max had a high-powered job and a house in Kensington. Jas could practically hear her mother drooling over the phone. She said they looked forward to meeting Max soon. He sounded just the kind of man they hoped she would marry and time was moving on—she wasn't getting any younger. A maternal reminder Jas didn't need to hear.

On Sunday she had wandered through the galleries at the Royal Academy and then meandered her way through the busy streets to the Savoy. Treating herself to tea on the terrace, she could pretend she was waiting for her tall, handsome lover. But the lover didn't turn up and she left, unful-filled.

Chapter Five

Break Out Sessions

So far it had been a frustrating morning for Den. Without the benefit of sat-nav in the car, she had been misdirected twice by locals. Perhaps they were truly ignorant, or just trying to protect their peaceful way of life.

She realised, belatedly, that she could have made life easier for herself by scoping out the site on Sunday. But she'd spent the day wavering between guilt at not visiting her parents who lived close by and obsessing over what had gone wrong between her and Kathryn. The rest of time she distracted herself with doing research on local history and playing computer games.

Once on the right road, she found the field easily. The long line of vehicles parked on the road near the farm was a sure sign of activity. One of the vans even had the Bournemouth University logo on it. Parking her car on the grass verge she trekked past the other cars to the farmhouse that, unlike Starling Hill, was on the roadside. A dog barked as she approached the front door.

The woman who answered her knock didn't look pleased to see her. Before Den had time to identify herself, she was told abruptly, "Go through the gate up the lane." And the door was slammed in her face.

The openness of the landscape made it possible to see the archaeological activity in a field on the other side of a large ploughed area. It looked like there were more excavators than there had been at Starling Hill but maybe this southern university had been able to throw more resources at it. From her research on the Internet the day before she had found reference to a BBC programme featuring earlier university-sponsored digs on this same site, referred to as the Big Dig. If they had already had television exposure, she didn't think they would object to a lone journalist taking an interest. It would be unlike her disastrous attempt to reach the Starling Hill site when she'd ended up spending an uncomfortable night on the moor before being shot at by an irate farmer. If Jas hadn't been concerned enough to contact Robin to find out why she hadn't called her, she wouldn't be here today. She was sure of that. Memories of that long night still haunted her.

Den took her camera out and quickly snapped a few photos. They wouldn't be used in the article but it helped to put the surrounding area in context. Leaving her laptop in the car wasn't an option, she decided, no matter how out of the way this location seemed. So, as well as her camera, she was carrying her shoulder bag. Still it didn't look too far to the dig site. Good thing she'd remembered to bring a sturdy pair of trainers because the terrain looked a bit rough. At least she'd learned something from her other archaeological site visits.

There was a car coming so she stepped in between the BU van and a large SUV to get out of the way. A flash of red blurred past and as she moved back onto the road she saw it slowing down to park up past the gate the woman at the farmhouse had told her to use. It couldn't be, could it? The fresh air had her hallucinating. The professor was at the other end of the country. But it looked like her car and as she got closer, there was no doubt—Kathryn was climbing out of it.

†

Nearing the site, Kathryn could feel excitement bubbling up inside her. The rolling countryside and open farmland was so different to the Yorkshire hills, valleys and vast areas of empty moorland. There was no comparison to the landscapes of the north that she was familiar with but she was looking forward to seeing the discoveries made at this villa. After dinner with the boys, she had spent an hour on the Internet researching the area. It was fascinating reading. The Durotriges tribe in that part of Dorset had been anti-Roman and, unlike the Queen of the Brigantes, their leaders did not welcome the invaders. The university's dig had been taking place over the last few years and had already added greatly to the knowledge of the transition from Iron Age to Roman use of the land.

Burials became more common with the rise in the acceptance of Christianity as the Empire's main religion. Before then, the Romans had mainly favoured cremation. Kathryn knew from her own research that although numerous Roman villas had been excavated throughout the country, the bones of their owners had never before been uncovered. This was mainly due to their belief system. They always buried the dead outside their settlements. The skeletons found at the site she was visiting had been put in a plot not far from the house, but there was evidence that it had been enclosed and was perhaps an early forerunner of the family tombs favoured in Victorian times. The grave goods uncovered during the excavations indicated the occupants of the villa were high status, possibly Roman citizens who inter-married and settled in an area undeveloped and rich in mineral deposits.

The ploughed fields she passed gave her pause for thought. It was an archaeologist's nightmare, the destruction of so much through intensive farming practices. Farmers had been finding pottery and coins for centuries without bothering to alert anyone. Who wanted the inconvenience of a full-fledged archaeological dig disrupting their way of life? At least, it seemed, this landowner had decided to give the experts the chance to excavate his site properly. Having a university with a reputable archaeology and anthropology department nearby had probably helped.

She had texted her contact when leaving Salisbury and he'd sent a message back saying he would meet her at the gate. She drove past the line of vehicles and parked on the grass verge by a low hedge. She changed into the hiking boots she always carried in the boot of the car. Prepared for a day in the sun she had applied sun cream when she stopped for a coffee break at a motorway services. Finally she put on her battered green bush hat, locked the car and set off for the entrance to the field.

The man at the gate she recognised from their previous meeting. He was looking down the road away from her. She glanced that way and had no difficulty identifying the approaching figure. There was no mistaking the tall form, dressed in her usual summer attire, low-slung jeans, sleeveless shirt, dark sunglasses, and, on this occasion, a baseball cap. Kathryn reached her colleague at the same time as Den. The man looked from one to the other. After a moment's confusion he acknowledged Kathryn and held his hand out to her.

"Dr Moss. Nice to see you again." He looked at Den and back to Kathryn again. "Um, do you two know each other?"

Den answered. "Yes. We worked together on the Starling Hill dig. I'm Denise Sullivan." She didn't look at Kathryn.

"Oh. Okay. Well, glad you're both here at the same time. It's a bit of a trek to the site."

Kathryn decided she would have to ignore Den for the time being since the journalist was avoiding eye contact with her anyway. She concentrated on the enthusiastic outpouring from her colleague. His description of the discovery of five skeletons in an enclosure near the villa was exciting enough for her to be able to distance herself emotionally from Den.

As they walked around the site, she was aware that Den was taking photos. Occasionally she asked a question and Kathryn guessed she was recording everything as she wasn't taking notes.

Invited to inspect the trenches and then view the main findings on their site computer, Kathryn was totally absorbed in the archaeology and didn't notice that Den had disappeared until the team stopped for lunch. She looked around and finally asked if the journalist was still there.

"No. She left some time ago. Said she needed to write up her notes but she's planning to come back again tomorrow. I've offered to give her the pick of the photos of the completed skeletons."

"Okay. Good. Is it okay if I stick around for a bit, though? It's absolutely fascinating."

"Yes, of course. It's great to be able to share this with you."

"I don't mind getting my hands dirty. Please put me to work."

She spent the afternoon on her knees, happily trowelling away, and chatting with the students working next to her. They were keen to tell her about their experiences and how the information gained on the dig was going to be useful for their dissertations. She encouraged them to talk, enjoying as she always did, contact with enquiring young minds.

It was after five when she left the site, having helped the group clear up their equipment and pack it into the van. She set off for the inn feeling both intellectually stimulated and bodily refreshed, deciding that after a shower and an early dinner she would probably manage another good night's sleep. She would find a way to talk to Den at the site the next day.

✝

Even with the slight increase in traffic through the small market town of Blandford Forum, the journey to the inn only took fifteen minutes. Kathryn removed her overnight bag from the boot of the car and ventured inside. It was an attractive building with low-beamed rooms and, delighting in the warm décor, she decided it had been a good find.

Showered and changed into a clean, fairly respectable tailored shirt and comfortable chinos, she made her way down to the bar. The barman suggested she might want to take her gin and tonic out to the garden behind the inn. It was a lovely warm evening and she ventured out to find a well-kept lawn with picnic tables dotted around. A lone guest with an almost empty pint glass, tapping away on a laptop, occupied only one of them. She gasped and almost dropped her drink.

Den turned around to face her.

"Well, well. Of all the inns in all the world…"

"It was the name of the village. I couldn't resist."

"Me neither." Den grinned at her and closed her laptop.

Kathryn took this as an invitation to join her, seating herself on the bench opposite.

"So, is this an amazing coincidence, or should I be flattered that you followed me here?" Den removed her sunglasses and gave her a searching look.

"Finding you here is a coincidence, but yes, I followed you. Henry told me about your assignment. It didn't take long to find out where it was. Archaeology is a fairly small community in this country."

"You've talked to Henry?"

"Yes, I stayed there last night."

Den closed her eyes for a moment and then stared back at Kathryn. "Did you stay in my room?"

"Yes. I slept in your bed and I remembered the last time I'd been there." Kathryn reached out to hold Den's hand.

She snatched it away. "Don't play games with me, Kathryn. You didn't want to know me a few days ago."

"I know. I'm sorry."

"It's a long way to come just to say 'sorry'."

"You weren't answering my calls."

"Well, now you know what it feels like. Why didn't you call me back before?"

Kathryn sighed. She took a long sip of her drink. All the thoughts that had haunted her during her sleepless nights had disappeared. Whole speeches she had rehearsed endlessly, vanished.

"I don't know," she said finally. "It was stupid. I knew I wanted the Durham job and I knew you wouldn't like it."

"That's a bit lame. Am I that hard to talk to?"

"No. It's me. I'm not good at this relationship business."

"Yeah, I'd noticed."

"Den." Kathryn reached across the table but Den kept her arms folded protectively across her chest. "I am really sorry about last week. Can you forgive me?"

"I thought I could until I saw how you were with Ellie."

"That's over."

"Is it?"

'Okay. I admit I'm still attracted to her. But she's married to Robin. And I'm moving to Durham. So, nothing's going to happen there."

"Great. Nice to know I'm second best."

"Jesus, Den. I like being with you. We've always been good together."

"That might be enough for you. But I'm struggling with it." Den finished the last of her beer and stood. "I'm going for a walk."

"Have dinner with me."

"Thanks. But I'll probably have room service. See you around." She picked up her laptop and stalked off.

Kathryn looked around at the scenery, not noticing the beauty of the garden, her eyes blurred with tears. It looked like another long, lonely night.

†

Den managed to avoid Kathryn all the next day. She had skipped breakfast, staying in her room to draft her article and arrived at the site midmorning. The professor was studying the drawings one of the students was making. If she was aware of Den's presence she didn't give any sign. After speaking to some of the volunteers and two of the university lecturers, she left. The lead archaeologist, who had shown them around the day before, emailed her two good photos of the skeletons in situ. The journalist felt she now had more than enough information for the article.

†

Driving around the country lanes and finding another small village pub by a river, Den tried to sort out her feelings for the professor. Going over the conversation in the garden the evening before she couldn't find anything to hang on to. Maybe Kathryn was more interested in the dig than in trying to rekindle their relationship. And what kind of relationship did she want? Just friends? A fuck buddy? She smiled grimly to herself. Kathryn wouldn't put it so crudely but it seemed that was exactly what she wanted.

102

Although she had already booked out of the inn she returned after her pub lunch to sit in the pleasant surroundings of their garden to finish off her article and use the free Wi-Fi to send it to Tom. With the quotes obtained in her morning visit to the dig added in and a selection of photos she felt her editor would be more than satisfied with her two days' work.

Phoning home she had spoken to Paul. He sounded groggy, having just woken up. She'd forgotten he was back on nights and that Henry was gone for the week. Paul told her in detail, more than she either wanted or asked for, about Kathryn's visit. How she had arrived looking shattered and had then slept all day.

"She must still be keen, D."

"I'm not so sure."

"Oh, come on. Give her a break. We thought she'd gone back up north Monday. We didn't know she was still trying to chase you down. That's so romantic." He somehow managed to stretch 'so' into a three-syllable word.

"I think it's called stalking."

"What's your problem, chick?"

"My problem? I'm not the one with a problem."

"Who are you kidding?"

Den had ended the call saying she was setting off soon but would stop somewhere for dinner on the way back. It was a safer option than relying on Paul to provide a decent meal, and he would be going to the gym before heading in to work so it was likely they would miss seeing each other anyway.

The sun disappeared behind a cloud heralding a chill to the air as she packed her laptop away and walked around to the car park. Kathryn pulled up just as she was closing the boot.

The professor slid out of the driver's seat quickly and walked over to her. "Please, Den. We need to talk." She was still wearing her bush hat and the dusty-looking cargo shorts that might have been clean two days ago. Her breasts were straining against the sweat-stained fabric of her T-shirt. Den found her libido responding automatically. She reached out and brushed a stray strand of hair away from Kathryn's mouth.

"All right. But not out here." She retrieved her laptop bag from the car and followed Kathryn up to her room.

†

The long Sunday stretched into an even longer Monday and Tuesday. Jasmine kept going over the events of the weekend and wondering what she had done wrong. Had she been too submissive? Did Max expect her to rebel? Or was this all part of the game, making her wait? She was fairly certain that calling Max was out of the question.

Tuesday afternoon she told Ray she had a meeting with another client and walked out of the office. At first she had planned to go to Starbucks and indulge in a full fat latte. But the memory of seeing herself in the floor-to-ceiling mirrors in Max's bedroom, reminded her that she was on a diet. She ordered an Americano and sat with her back to the wall. The Wi-Fi signal was good so she Googled the name of the shop Den had told her about after the educational foray into Ann Summers. The address on the website was Hoxton Square. It was a good taxi ride away but she thought she could get away with claiming it on her expenses.

She asked the taxi driver to drop her by the gardens. She didn't want him knowing her business. Walking around the corner the pink banners outside the shop didn't look too intimidating but she walked past a few times before going in. She wished Den were with her. Once inside the range of items on display amazed her. It all looked very bright and cheerful and less intimidating than she had expected.

Ten minutes later she was standing outside with her purchase. The helpful sales assistant had shown her how it worked and had even included the batteries. She could hear Den's laughter if she told her about this. *How do you get to your age without ever having owned a dildo?*

Well, whether or not she heard from Max, she was going to get some satisfaction this evening.

✝

The roads were clear until she reached the outskirts of the city. Den tried hard not to think of the sleeping woman she'd left as dawn was breaking over the soft Dorset hills. Soft as a woman's breasts. No, it wasn't sensible to go there while she was driving. The shuffle god's sense of humour played kd lang singing "I Wish I Didn't Love You So" followed by "Constant Craving". Den pulled the plug on the iPod before the song ended. Her own thoughts were engaged in a battle to forget what her body had been doing a few hours before.

They hadn't talked much, barely making it to the room before tearing at each other's clothes. The simple touch of Kathryn's lips on hers and Den was on fire. When Kathryn reached between her legs, the wetness meeting her hand was all the invitation the professor needed to drag her over to the bed. Every time she made love with Kathryn she was baffled by the contrasts in her personality. The cold, aloof professional disappeared and morphed into a sexually skilled and demanding partner. Maybe she was, as Ellie had said, capable of putting her feelings into boxes, cataloguing them and pulling them out only when she needed to examine them more closely. Maybe Den was just one of her 'finds' that excited her interest on occasion, taken out, inspected, and put back in the box.

105

So much had been left unspoken during the night of passion. Late in the evening, when a different hunger announced itself with their stomachs rumbling in unison, Kathryn had ordered a meal from room service. Omelette and chips with a side salad and rolls. Den waited in the bathroom until the waiter had gone. In London they wouldn't have bothered to be so discreet. But this was a small community and there was no point in frightening the locals.

While they ate, sharing the meal, Den asked what Kathryn's plans were for the summer. She said she would be going up to Durham the following week to spend some time on the Binchester site, a university-sponsored dig. The finds at the Roman fort there were gaining in significance but in her opinion still had some way to go before capturing the imagination the way the Vindolanda writing tablets had. Nevertheless the archaeology was proving to be important enough to gain some media attention. She suggested Den come up if she could convince her editor there was a story worth pursuing. Den pointed out that he wasn't likely to splash out for more expenses after this little trip. Kathryn said she could stay with her and help with the house hunting she would be doing in her spare time.

When she talked about the work she would be doing at Binchester she became animated. "It's my world, Den. I want to share it with you. Why don't you just take some time off and come up for a few weeks? It's great fun. You've seen it here and up there the mix of volunteers is amazing, people from all over the world, all walks of life. As well as the staff and students from our university, there's a group over from the States taking part in the excavation."

Not wanting to destroy the moment, Den had said she would think about it. She noted that Kathryn was already referring to Durham University in a possessive tone, *our university*. In her mind, it seemed, she was already there.

They had washed down the last few chips with the small bottle of white wine from the minibar and returned to bed. After another round of intense lovemaking, they both slipped into sleep, arms wrapped around each other. Den loved the closeness, holding the warm body, feeling her lover's heart beating against her chest. She lay still for a while after waking in the early hours, savouring the musky scent surrounding them. It took her a few minutes to slowly and carefully extricate herself without disturbing Kathryn's deep sleep.

†

Returning the car and waiting while the attendant checked for any damage, Den considered her choices. Fighting her way down the steps of the tube station, past the paper pushers—the Metro, Big Issue, and recently the Watchtower, Jehovah's Witnesses having decided that stopping busy commuters might be a more effective method of recruitment than door-stepping people at home—or taking a taxi and adding the fare to her list of expenses. The taxi won.

The house was quiet, as she had expected. Paul would be sleeping and Steph already out at work. She put the kettle on and checked the fridge. Any calories she had ingested during her last meal shared with Kathryn had dissipated during their night of energetic lovemaking. It looked like toast and jam was the only menu option. There was enough milk for a few cups of coffee. Paul was a sweet guy and no doubt a terrific ward nurse, but he wasn't a good housekeeper. They only ate well when Henry was at home.

She flicked through the main section of the newspaper. Henry had one delivered even though he wasn't there most weeks to enjoy it. Den saved articles for him while he was away and she noticed yesterday's paper was lying on a chair unopened.

Her phone rang—Kathryn's face lit up the smartphone's screen. She had been expecting the call and had only hoped the professor wouldn't wake up too soon and call her while she was driving. Den knew she should have told her she had to leave early but somehow hadn't been able to find the words during the night. Kathryn was fired up about her new job during the one conversation they did have and after that her mouth was otherwise engaged as they lost themselves in the taste of each other's bodies.

"Hey," she said.

"Hey, yourself. Where are you?"

"I'm home."

"Home, as in home in London?"

"Yes, Professor. That's what home means."

Silence on the other end. Den waited.

"I thought you would be here. I wanted to wake up with you."

"Mmm. That would have been nice. But I had to return the car."

"Oh. I thought it was yours."

"I've never owned a car. It was a staff car and they wanted it back today for someone else to use."

"Den?"

"Yes."

"Last night…there were things I wanted to say."

"Okay."

"You're not going to make this easy for me, are you?"

"You never make things easy, Kat."

"Have you been up to your room, yet?"

"No. I'm in the kitchen having coffee and toast."

"I left you a note. Read it. Then call me back, please. I'll be on the road most of the day, but will be home by this evening."

Den noted the uncertainty in Kathryn's voice, a pleading tone almost. Was this the breakthrough she'd been hoping for? Had the professor finally cracked open one of her boxes. The one labelled 'love'.

She promised to ring her, ending the call as she made her way slowly up the stairs to her room.

†

Kathryn glanced around, making sure she hadn't left anything behind. Even though she had showered she could still smell the tantalising odour of their lovemaking. She picked up her bag and shut the door on the memories of the night. The disappointment of waking up to find Den gone was still raw. And her lover's unemotional tone when she called hadn't helped to calm the overwhelming sense of loss. If this was what it was like to be in love she wasn't sure she could handle it.

A few deep breaths of the fresh country air as she walked out to her car brought a sense of perspective. It was another beautiful day and she had a long drive ahead. There were many things to think about. Packing for the three weeks she was planning to spend in Durham, photographs to be sorted for the Cartimandua exhibition, and the task she was dreading—house hunting. She was still debating whether or not to just get a small flat and rent out the house in Lindley, for a few years at least.

Archaeology wasn't a secure or lucrative career option and although some universities were able to attract the requisite number of students for their courses, the numbers were dropping each year. Obtaining funding for digs was getting harder and many sites were dependent on volunteers who were willing to pay for the privilege of scraping around in the dirt for a few weeks in the hopes of finding something of significance. She knew her own digging days were probably

109

limited. Although still fit and healthy and hoping to be able to keep on with fieldwork as long as she could, there would come a time in the not too distant future when her body would object to the long hours doing trench work.

Checking her map again, she decided to make the slight detour to visit the site known as Vespasian's Camp, near Stonehenge. She knew the misnamed site had nothing to do with the Roman emperor but it was yielding some fascinating discoveries, leading archaeologists to believe that the evidence of early occupation going back nine thousand years explained why Stonehenge was where it was, although the mysteries of how it had been built and for what purpose remained unsolved.

Once she reached Newbury it was rush hour and Kathryn knew it would add some time to her journey. The stop-and-go traffic on this particular stretch of road brought to mind the 1996 protests about clearing the land for a new bypass. She thought it ironic that aggregate for the new road came from the nearby decommissioned RAF Greenham Common base. That led to the memory of her mother telling her not so long ago that her one regret in life was that she hadn't taken part in the Women's Peace Camp outside the base. Kathryn had difficulty imagining her mother living in a tent, eating out of tins, and enduring all the other discomforts of life outdoors. She probably wouldn't have lasted more than one night before deserting the sisterhood to book into a hotel and find the nearest golf course.

She kept looking at her phone, willing it to ring. But then she thought that if Den really wanted a proper discussion with her, she would call in the evening. When she thought about what was in the letter she had left in Den's room, she wondered if she would hear from the journalist at all. She should, perhaps, have phoned Henry and asked him to rip it up before Den arrived home.

After an hour at the Camp in Amesbury she made her next stop Oxford. A leisurely lunch at the Randolph Hotel followed by a quick stroll through a few galleries at the Ashmolean Museum and she was on her way again. The long boring stretch up the M1 and a stop for coffee at the crowded Leicester Forest East services didn't improve her mood.

It was around seven o'clock by the time Kathryn turned into her driveway. She'd been on the road for going on eleven hours and was looking forward to opening a bottle of Australian red she had been saving for a special occasion.

With the premonition of a headache coming on she would probably manage an evening of staring at a World Cup football match with the sound off. Whether Den phoned or not didn't really matter now, she decided. She was too exhausted to care.

✝

"Armadillo Press Office." Ray was answering the phone on her desk as she arrived. "Sorry, she's not here at the moment. Oh no, hold on, she's just walked in."

Ray handed her the receiver, a big grin plastered on his face. "I think it's Max Fleetwood."

Jasmine grabbed the phone from him and waved him away. "I could murder a coffee, sweetie." She hoped her face wasn't giving away her excitement. Luckily, he just nodded and went out.

"Hello," she said as calmly as she could manage with her heart pounding.

Max's sexy purr came through the phone line. "Are you hot, darling?"

"Slightly warm, yes."

"I think your delicious buns need heating up."

Jas squirmed in her chair. "Um, yes. I think they do."

"Good. Tonight. Seven. My place."

"Yes, okay." Jas found it hard to swallow.

Ray arrived back with her coffee as Max continued with her instructions. "Wear your black dress, no panties." And with that she was gone. Jasmine put the receiver down carefully and looked up at Ray.

"So, what did she want?" he asked.

"Just checking we're on schedule with the press releases for next week."

"She could have asked me that. Anyway, I sent Roisin the copy through while you were out."

"Well, I guess that's how she got to where she is. It pays to be thorough."

"What's in the bag?"

Jas realised, with horror, that she'd dumped her shopping on the desk in her haste to get to the phone. "Oh, just a little something for a friend's birthday." Thankfully, the bag was a plain white one. She didn't want to have to explain to her assistant why she'd had to go out in the middle of the day to visit a sex shop and certainly not one that advertised itself as a women's erotic emporium.

"Right. Well, there are a few more messages for you. I put them on email."

"Okay. Thanks. I'll have a look."

Jas waited for Ray to leave then sat back in her chair and took a few deep breaths. This was the call she'd been waiting for. Getting through the next few hours exhibiting any degree of normality was going to prove difficult.

†

Den stared at the envelope sitting in the centre of her desk. No hearts and flowers, nothing fancy, just her name on the outside. She paced around her room, noting the tidiness. Henry's doing, or Kathryn's. Or both.

She unpacked her bag and threw some things on the floor to give it a more homely look. Did she want to read Kathryn's note now? All she really wanted was to go to sleep. The emotional turmoil of the last few days and the drive back from Dorset were taking their toll. It would take Kathryn a good five hours or more to get home and she could only do that driving without a break. She was sure to stop off somewhere. Oxford, most likely, as it was on the way.

The envelope looked thick. More than one sheet of paper. Typical academic, she thought. Probably had footnotes and a bibliography. Well, whatever it said, it could wait. Sleep first and then a shower. If she showered now it would only disturb Paul. And he needed his sleep after a night on the wards.

Lying down on her bed, sleep eluded her. When she closed her eyes, she saw Kathryn's body in the afterglow of her orgasm, blue eyes unfocused and a radiant smile illuminating her face. Caressing that body again in her mind, kissing her lips, tongue searching out the sensitive spots, Den moaned as her fingers sought her own wet opening. Gasping, gripping the duvet with her free hand as she came, she marvelled again at the fierceness of her desire for the professor. She was certain she'd never felt this overwhelming passion for anyone else before. Not even in her hormonally charged teenage years. Whoever said women's sex drive peaked in their twenties or thirties was full of crap.

She woke up to find she'd slept for five hours. Taking a deep breath the aroma hit her. If she'd ever been in a brothel, it would probably smell like this. Getting up slowly, she opened a window. Her glance caught sight of the envelope. *Okay. Shower first, then read it.*

After the shower, feeling refreshed, dressed in clean shorts and T-shirt, she picked up the envelope and went downstairs. The sun was out and it seemed like a good idea to read it in the garden, letting her hair dry naturally, with a glass of something cold.

✝

Paul was in the kitchen making a sandwich. "Hey, you're back. Do you want one?" He indicated the bread and cheese.

"Yeah, thanks."

"I'll be glad when Hen gets back. My cholesterol levels will be through the roof."

Den laughed. She knew Paul lived on cheese while Henry was away. Although, occasionally he had been known to open a can of tuna.

"So, did you and Dr Moss…you know?"

"Yes, we did."

"Oh good. I do like a happy ending." He handed her a sandwich. "What? Oh, you want a plate, you know where they are."

"When does Henry get back?" She fetched two plates from the cupboard and passed him one.

"Friday."

"Right. So, is it takeaway or the pub this evening?"

"Since you're going to take me out and tell me a tale of love and lust in deepest Dorset, it's the pub."

She put her sandwich on a plate and fetched two beers from the fridge.

"What's that?" he asked when they were sitting outside with their food and drink.

"What?" She looked down to where he was pointing. The envelope was sticking out of her pocket. "Oh, that. It's something Kathryn wants me to read. She left it in my room on Monday."

"Ooh. A love letter! Haven't you looked at it yet?"

"No."

114

"Christ. I'd be dying of curiosity. Hell, I am dying of curiosity. Do you want me to open it? I could read it to you."

"Fuck off. It's my letter. I'll read it when I'm ready."

"I'm ready now." He snatched the envelope out of her pocket.

"Paul, give it back."

He waved it above his head, out of her reach. "It feels like a hefty tome. An essay, perhaps? More than an ode to love."

"Paul!"

Something in her tone warned him to quit playing around. He grinned sheepishly and handed the envelope back. "Please don't hurt me."

"Get lost and let me read it in peace."

"Okay, okay." He collected their empty plates and glasses and headed back into the kitchen. A few minutes later the sound of his new favourite boy band, Stornoway, came blaring out of the speakers through the open windows in the nearby dining room. She couldn't help smiling at his choice. The first song, "Zorbing", was unrelentingly cheerful and uplifting. A summer song extolling the joys of summer love.

Den took the envelope and studied her name printed on the front. Not much to read into the three letters scrawled there. Regret, misery, desire. She lifted the flap, not glued down. Henry could have read it already, she thought. Two A4 pages, folded precisely into thirds. Plain paper, taken from her printer stock. The handwritten words were neatly printed, not a cursive script. Den realised the only time she had seen the professor holding a pen was when she was labelling bags of finds. Still, at least it was legible. She wondered if there had been earlier drafts and this was the clean copy, neatly written, with no crossings out or notes in the margin.

Chapter Six

Project Research

Ellie glanced around the gallery, appreciating the light and the space that helped to show off her work to great effect. The timing of the exhibition couldn't be better. As Helen, the gallery owner, had put it, "the increased footfall through the town for the Tour de France, it will be *magnifique, cherie!*" Helen had lived in Yorkshire for twenty years and was married to an Englishman but at times she could sound very French. And the preparations for the Tour de France stage coming through Hebden Bridge had intensified her nationalistic fervour as well as her accent.

There was nothing more she could do. All the pictures, bar one, were in place, the tables set up for drinks and canapés. The paint was barely dry on the final canvas and she still wasn't sure she wanted to display it at the open evening. Robin had suggested she keep it in reserve and put it up when one of the others had sold, and it was an idea she was seriously considering.

The concept for the painting had come to her after Kathryn's visit and Den's blurted revelation that Queen Cartimandua had lived out her days at Starling Hill with her female lover. The press would undoubtedly sensationalise the news. The Queen of the Brigantes tribe, the Sappho of the North. They would love it. Ellie, as an historian, knew that the tribal customs of the time embraced sexual relations between women as no less natural than with men. Sex with men was necessary for procreation but it didn't mean a woman had to stay with a man for life. Women in Britain enjoyed a more equal status than women in Rome. This changed over time as the Roman way of life took hold and the introduction of Christianity certainly finished off any freedoms women had previously enjoyed.

Taking one last look round, she found Helen counting glasses in the back room. "I'll be back in a while. Just going to the flat to get changed."

Helen nodded and carried on counting.

✝

Ellie let herself out into the alleyway leading onto the main street. It was only a short walk to the holiday apartment Helen had made available to them for the weekend. The building was one of the properties run by her husband and it was fortunate that it was available as everywhere in town was fully booked by the cycling enthusiasts. All the surrounding roads were closing for the race on Sunday and Helen had wanted to be able to keep the gallery open on the day with the expected influx of visitors.

"I'm home, sweetheart," she called, the aroma of freshly brewed coffee assaulting her nostrils. Robin appeared in the doorway to the kitchen and leant against the frame. Ellie licked her lips at the sight of her partner wearing only a pair of tight-fitting briefs and a smile. They had been married for all of two months now and still couldn't seem to get enough of each other.

She moved slowly towards her. "I have to get showered and dressed."

117

"Mmm. So, you'll have to get undressed first." Robin closed the distance between them with one easy stride and embraced her.

"Rob, I don't have time." Ellie squirmed as Robin's tongue circled her earlobe. "The show opens at seven."

"That's two hours from now." Robin captured her lips, effectively stopping her from mouthing any further protest. Powerless to move, pressed up against the wall with one of her lover's arms bracing her neck and the other opening her blouse to gain access to her breasts, Ellie moaned and knew she was losing this battle.

Two hours later she was frantically brushing her hair and applying last-minute touches to her makeup. "Helen's going to kill me for being late."

"This is Hebden Bridge, hon." Robin had already dressed and made an attempt to flatten her hair. "Everyone will be late. Anyway, it only takes two minutes to get there."

"Do I look all right?"

"You look more than all right. If I didn't have to go to this damn open evening, I'd take you to bed, again." Robin grinned.

It was the seductive grin that always made Ellie's insides melt. Robin was looking very sexy in her tailored black chinos and green and white striped shirt, open at the collar.

"I think the artist might be expecting you to escort her to this damn open evening."

Robin held her arm out. "Come along, then, Miss Artist. We don't want to keep your public waiting."

†

Kathryn hadn't been sure what to expect. The piece in the paper had been brief and she only noticed it because she'd been looking through to check on rental prices in the area. She was still undecided on whether to rent her house out or take the plunge and sell up. The small photo of Ellie caught her eye with the wording next to it advertising an open evening showcasing the work of local artist and potter, Eleanor Winters.

The last few days had passed agonisingly slowly. Den still hadn't responded to her letter. She had been over their last conversation and couldn't think why the journalist was being so obtuse. Their night together in Dorset had been warm and loving, once they got past the initial frantic clash of desires. Maybe there was something she was missing. Why had Den slipped away before dawn, leaving her without a word? It didn't fit with the declaration of love she'd given her before. Well, it was up to her to make the next move. Kathryn had other things on her mind. She was going to Durham Saturday to view an apartment that looked like it might be suitable. She had checked it out online and it was in a small block of modern-looking flats overlooking the river. Much as she loved her house, it would be a relief to leave the emotional turmoil behind.

✝

Kathryn drove into the valley and followed the road to the old mill town. Parking proved to be more difficult than she had thought and she drove around the streets several times before finding a car park with a few empty spaces. Luckily this meant she had spotted the gallery's location as she passed it twice and was able to walk to it easily. The building had undoubtedly once been one of the town's thriving mills and the large windows on the upper floor provided an ideal space for an art gallery.

What she wasn't prepared for was the impact Ellie's paintings had on her. Pottery didn't interest her much. The potsherds that turned up on every dig she'd ever been involved in were valued as evidence of the kind of lives lived in each location. Ellie produced nice-looking pottery that would adorn people's kitchens but to her mind they were nothing special. Seeing the paintings, though, the dramatic use of colour and light to bring a landscape to life, Kathryn wondered why Ellie hadn't embarked on this career sooner.

There were a few people walking around stopping to look at the displayed pictures. She spotted Ellie talking to someone by the buffet table. Caught out once again by the strength of her feelings for this woman, she stood to one side watching her. Surely she was too old for this kind of school-girl crush. Her heart was pounding so loudly she was sure everyone in the room could hear it. Maybe Den was right and she wasn't ready to commit herself fully to their relationship. Drinking in the sight of Ellie looking as beautiful as she always did in her dreams, wearing a simple strapless summer dress that clung to her curves like a limpet.

"Enjoying the view, Professor?"

Kathryn turned to find Robin glaring at her. Ellie's partner was looking better than the last time she'd seen her at the farm. She cleaned up well and was actually looking quite smart for once. The green on her shirt accentuated the colour of her eyes and complemented her reddish brown hair.

"Just looking," she said as calmly as she could.

"Fine. As long as you're just looking. The pictures are on the walls though."

Unable to think of a suitable retort that wouldn't sound rude, Kathryn just nodded. Whatever Robin was working up to saying was forestalled by another woman arriving and grabbing Robin from behind.

"Hey, Rob. Good to see you." She kissed a startled Robin on the cheek.

The newcomer was dressed in a flowing caftan with matching headscarf that she may have made herself. It only took a moment for Kathryn to recall her from her visits to

Starling Hill. One of Ellie's pottery students, Jo Moon Face or something equally hippy dippy. Didn't these people know the Age of Aquarius was long gone?

"Professor Moss. Great to see you too." Thankfully the woman didn't attempt to kiss her. "What are you doing in these parts?" She carried on speaking without waiting for an answer. "Aren't Ellie's paintings wonderful?"

"Yes. I just got here. I'm going to have a look around." Kathryn moved away, quickly walking over to the furthest corner and found herself looking at a vision. It was a view of Starling Hill she knew only too well. The sun coming up over the horizon casting an orange glow over the moorland. However, unlike the other pictures in the exhibition, this one had two people in it. Two women. One tall, dark-haired, wearing recognisably Roman armour, with her arm around a slightly shorter blonde woman with a golden torque around her neck. They were watching the sunrise, the light on their faces, turned slightly away towards the glowing landscape.

"Beautiful, isn't it"

Kathryn looked at the speaker who had moved up quietly to stand by her side. "Yes."

"Helen Chandler." The woman extended her hand.

"Kathryn Moss. This is your gallery?" It wasn't a question she needed answered. The name was on the sign outside.

"*Oui*. I'm very pleased to be able to show Ellie's work. She's a talented artist."

"Yes. Is this picture for sale?" Kathryn had noticed that all the other paintings had prices along with their descriptions on cards on the wall.

"I don't know. Ellie wasn't going to display it but I managed to persuade her at the last minute."

"Does it have a title?"

"I didn't have time to make up a card, but…"

"I'm sure Dr Moss doesn't need a description." Ellie was standing at her elbow.

Kathryn breathed in her scent and wondered if she could control herself. She wanted to pull her into her arms, feel her warm breasts pressing up against her own, taste her lips, kissing her deeply.

"What are you doing here?" Ellie hissed. Fortunately, the proprietor had moved away to speak to another viewer.

"I saw the ad in the paper. Just wanted to see your work. It's good, Ellie. It's better than good. It's brilliant." Kathryn knew she was babbling but couldn't help it. Ellie's closeness had that effect on her. "This painting's amazing. You've really captured the essence of how I imagined the two of them. It has power and presence. I would like to buy it."

"It's not for sale."

"Well, I would buy it if it was."

Startled by the presence of another visitor, Kathryn turned her head and was surprised to see her now former colleague. She couldn't believe her eyes.

"Ed! What are you doing here?" She found herself echoing Ellie's words to her moments ago.

"Kieran told me about this evening, so we've come over together. He and Elise are getting the drinks." He placed an arm easily around Ellie's bare shoulders. And Ellie didn't seem to mind the close contact. "Miss Winters never ceases to amaze me with her talents."

Kieran Taylor and Ed's wife, Elise, joined them then. Kieran handed Ed a glass of red wine. "Would you like a drink, Dr Moss?" he asked.

"No thanks. I won't be staying long."

"I thought you were in Durham anyway," Ed said, sipping at his wine.

"I'm going up tomorrow. Sorting out somewhere to live." Kathryn followed Ellie with her eyes as she moved away from their group. After a few minutes of exchanging pleasantries with Ed and Elise, she excused herself, and casting one last look at the painting, managed to make her exit without speaking to anyone else.

†

Den was genuinely puzzled by the contents of the letter Kathryn had left for her to read. It didn't make a lot of sense. The first page contained only a few lines of neatly printed out words. She expressed a desire to keep seeing Den and thought they could manage a long-distance relationship, if that's what Den wanted. The second page was a diagram, a drawing. Den wasn't even sure which way up it was supposed to be.

A long-distance relationship wasn't exactly what she wanted. She wanted someone to wake up next to, someone who would be there in the evening and at weekends. Someone to share life with, not just snatched sexual encounters. Although she enjoyed her London lifestyle, she knew it wasn't a fit with the professor's way of life. If anyone had to make the move, it was going to have to be her.

Kathryn had suggested she join her in Durham for the next few weeks she would be spending up there. The problem was she couldn't imagine herself living so far from the capital. Okay, so it was only a few hours on the train. It just seemed like the end of the world—the opposite end of her known universe. She tried phoning Jas to talk to her but just got her voice mail. Probably tied up, literally. And Henry was up in the air somewhere.

The only bright spot in her week was the praise from Tom, her editor. He was pleased with the article on the Dorset dig and asked her to provide some more background on the Durotriges tribe. She finished that Friday morning and went into the office to talk to him about a new assignment.

123

"It's just another bloody fort. Nothing new there. Up to here with fucking Roman forts."

"C'mon, Tom. I wouldn't mention it if Dr Moss hadn't said there was a lot going on up there. Archaeologists are calling it the 'Pompeii of the North'. That sounds intriguing to me."

"You want me to pay for another jaunt in the country-side?"

"I'll take the train."

"I'm not convinced. Sorry. No go."

"Fine. Well, I was thinking of taking a break. Looks like we'll be having some good weather for a bit. See you in a few weeks."

He hadn't protested, much.

Her next task was proving harder to accomplish.

"Please, pretty please! I'll look after it, honest." Den put on her best ingratiating smile. Henry was still sitting with his arms folded across his chest, expressionless. He had only landed back home an hour earlier and she had taken the earliest opportunity to approach him. "Give me a break, Dad. I could take the train, but after what happened last time, I would like to be independent." He was making her feel seventeen again and having to ask permission to use the family car.

Henry broke his silence, saying calmly, "You want to take my pride and joy up to the wilds of Northumberland."

"It's County Durham, actually."

"Is this to impress the girlfriend?" He even managed to sound like her father.

"I don't think I can call Kathryn a girlfriend, even if she was my girlfriend."

Henry finally broke into a smile. "Of course you can take it. It needs a good run anyway. I haven't used it since Paul and I went for that weekend in Rye."

Den punched his arm. "You bastard! You enjoyed making me beg, didn't you?"

"Just a bit. Anyway, it's all in a good cause. Only don't fuck it up, again. I can't take much more of this melodrama."

"I haven't fucked it up. It's this long-distance thing. I'm not sure I can do it."

"You'll find a way. Give it a chance. Paul and I manage even though I'm away so much and he works stupid shifts."

"And he trusts that you're not screwing your co-pilot on your aptly named layovers?"

"Well, not since my co-pilot's a woman. Now, the male steward, that's another matter." He grinned at her but she knew he was joking. He and Paul were devoted to each other.

Henry saw her off the next morning after making her eat a cooked breakfast. He also gave her a packed lunch and several bottles of mineral water. "Stop for a rest when you need to but don't eat any of the service station rubbish."

"I'm not going to the North Pole. And, anyway, I'm going to drop by Starling Hill to see Robin and Ellie."

"Well, text me when you get there, otherwise I'll be worried."

"About me or the car?"

"The car, obviously."

†

Den was still smiling as she eased the BMW onto the motorway. It was a lovely vehicle to drive and she was sure Henry would be concerned until she managed to return it safely. With it being the peak holiday period she had left early and managed to make good time on the roads. She was glad the car had built-in sat-nav as she wasn't sure she would have remembered how to get to Starling Hill on her own.

Driving into the yard she noted that Robin's bike was there, under cover, but the Jeep was gone. There was another car parked by the stables that she didn't recognise. As she got out and locked up, a voice called, "Hello!"

There was a man standing in the doorway to the pottery studio. She vaguely remembered him from her previous visits. Name of Kevin or something like that.

"Hi." She walked over to him and held out her hand. "Denise Sullivan. I don't know if you remember me."

"Oh, I remember you all right. Caused a lot of trouble with those stories of yours."

"Well, yeah. But it worked out okay in the end."

"Not before causing our Ellie a lot of grief."

"Hey, look. I'm sorry. Ellie and I are friends now. And it's her and Robin I've come to see. Are they here?"

"No, as it happens. I'm looking after the farm until they get back on Monday."

"Where are they, then?"

"Ellie's paintings are on show at a gallery in Hebden Bridge. The opening was last night and they're staying for the weekend. All the roads around here will be closed tomorrow for the cycle race."

"Oh, right."

"I went to the opening last night. Her artwork is stunning. Oh, and your professor was there."

"My professor?"

"Yes, the archaeologist. She was talking to Ellie when we arrived."

Den wished a hole in the ground would open up.

"She seemed to be interested in buying one of the paintings. Anyway, she didn't stay long. Said she was going up to Durham today."

Den looked over towards the field. Everything looked calm and peaceful but her insides were churning. She looked back at the man. Kieran, that was his name.

"What's the name of the art gallery, Kieran? They took me there last week but I didn't take note."

"Some French name. I've got a flyer in the house with the details if you're thinking of going there."

"Well, it's not far, is it? I would like to see Ellie's paintings. I only got a quick look when I was here before."

He seemed to lighten up as she showed an interest in Ellie's work. They walked over to the house together and he invited her in for a drink. She declined but asked if she could use the toilet. Despite Henry's best advice, she hadn't stopped for a break on the drive up, wanting to take advantage of the clear run.

Arc de Lumiere. Even with her mostly forgotten GCSE-level French she knew that meant arc of light. The flyer listed the proprietor as Helen Chandler. Not particularly French-sounding but she recalled the woman Ellie introduced her to had a slight accent.

She drove over to the other valley; again relying on the sat-nav. When Ellie drove them there on her last visit she hadn't been paying any attention to the route. The electronic directions, however, weren't much help with locating a place to park and she ended up on a side street with very narrow access. Henry would kill her if there were any scratches on his exquisite motor. Not for the first time that day, she wished it wasn't white. Every bit of dust showed up on it.

Having noted the location of the pub where they'd had lunch, she managed to navigate her way on foot to the gallery without much difficulty. Midday on a Saturday, though, and the town was heaving. It was like trying to fight your way down Oxford Street with people spilling out onto the roads where the pavement was too crowded. She missed getting run over several times by rampant cyclists who seemed to be everywhere.

There were quite a few people milling about in the gallery when she arrived. It looked like Ellie's artwork was attracting a fair amount of attention. One picture at the far end had a group gathered around it. She joined them. And stared. This was undoubtedly the painting Kathryn would want to buy. And other visitors seemed magnetically drawn to it. She gazed at it for a while, entranced by the power of the imagery.

"Oh, hello. I thought I recognised you."

Den tore her eyes away from the painting, momentarily disoriented.

"You're Ellie's friend from London."

It was the owner, Helen, standing at her elbow. She looked down at her. "Yes. I was hoping to see Ellie. Is she here?"

"Not at the moment. She's staying nearby though."

Five minutes later, Den found herself standing outside the apartment building. It looked newer than the others in the small square. She rang the doorbell for the number she'd been given and just when she was thinking they might not be in, Robin's voice came through the intercom. She identified herself and a short buzz followed, giving her access to the lift. Robin met her when the doors opened on the top floor wearing a T-shirt and shorts that looked like they were hastily put on. Her hair was standing up on end.

"Hey, good to see you!" She pulled her into an enthusiastic hug. "You should have let us know you were coming. Could have met you at the station."

"It was sort of spur of the moment and I drove up."

"I didn't know you had a car."

"I don't. I borrowed my housemate's."

"Well, come on in. This is a great place."

"How did you land this?"

"The building belongs to Bob Chandler, Helen's husband. She reserved it for us, and the timing's brilliant. We'll have a great view of the race from the balcony."

Ellie was coming out of another room into the lounge when they walked in. Den was pretty sure she had interrupted something.

"I'm sorry." Den could feel her face getting red. She edged back towards the door. "I guess I should have phoned."

"Don't be silly. I'm sure Rob can remember where we left off." Ellie smirked knowingly at her partner. "And we were just going to have lunch anyway."

✝

After the Wednesday night session with Max, Jasmine had been looking forward to Friday night. Sitting for any length of time was still uncomfortable but the accompanying twinges of pleasure made up for any lingering pain. And the bruises were yellowing out a bit. She had to twist around to see the neatly placed strokes across her butt in the mirror. With Max's words of praise still floating in her ears, telling her she was good, very good, Jasmine could feel herself getting wet again. It was a regular occurrence now and she'd taken to wearing full-strength pads to absorb the moisture. She had to change them several times during the day while she was at work, conscious of the smell of her arousal pervading the small office. Ray had commented on the pot of pine-scented potpourri now adorning her desk. She told him she liked the fresh woody odour.

She would have liked to be able to talk to someone about what she was feeling. With a sense of guilt she realised she hadn't spoken to Den all week and hadn't given her friend a thought even though she was suffering with her own relationship problems. But Den had housemates to talk to. Jas couldn't think of one acquaintance she would be able to share any of this with. It would be like coming out and it wasn't like she had any experience with that. The only people she had come out to were other lesbians. And then only when she was sure they were never likely to meet her parents.

Getting ready to meet Max. The box lay open on her bed. The box that had been delivered by courier to the office. She flushed at the thought of what would have happened if she hadn't been in to sign for it. Ray would have opened it thinking it was something important. Something he could deal with in her absence. Fortunately for her she had been there.

The printed instructions were simple. Wear this. Meet me at the club. Ten p.m. She had felt a sharp pang of disappointment that there would be no foreplay at Max's house before going to the club. However, she knew the rules. It was not for her to question why? She would do as she was told.

†

Robin thought the journalist was looking better than when she had seen her off on the train, amazingly only a week ago. Over lunch, Den had brought them up to date with the events of the past few days.

"So, you haven't called her?" Ellie asked.

"I know we'll end up arguing. I'll say something I'll regret. She's happy to keep me at arm's length. Her note made that clear. And the drawing doesn't make any sense at all. You'd think an academic could do a better job of communicating."

"I wouldn't count on it. They're generally living in another world." Ellie gave her a sympathetic look.

"So, let's take a look at this drawing then." Robin still felt twinges of jealousy whenever the professor's name was mentioned. She could feel her presence in the room.

130

"Rob, it's private!" Ellie squeezed her lover's knee.

"I might as well show you. I don't understand it." Den reached into the back pocket of her jeans and took out a folded sheet of paper. She handed it to Ellie.

Robin leant over to see what was on the page as Ellie unfolded it. "Looks like a treasure map."

Ellie studied it thoughtfully. "You might have something there, sweetheart." She looked up at Den. "She's drawn out all the elements of her life that are important to her. Look, see this tree with the roots going down into the earth. That represents her family. She's close to her father. There's her house, made out of books. And this big bit in the middle, the oblongs are trenches and the round things I thought might be postholes, but they could also indicate finds. But this is the important bit. Layers of earth and a heart in a locked box. The object next to it is a trowel." She smiled. "That is your mission, Den, should you choose to accept it. You have to scrape away the layers carefully to reveal the love that's been hidden, not for centuries in this case, but decades possibly."

"It's not buried that deep. She thinks she's in love with you." Den's voice was tinged with bitterness.

Robin shifted uncomfortably. She had been tempted to practice her boxing moves on Kathryn when she showed up at the gallery the night before. It was fortunate that Jo had turned up and defused the situation; putting a hand on her arm Jo said quietly, "She's no threat, Robin. She never has been. Let it go." However, she thought now that Den's assessment was spot-on. The way Kathryn had been looking at Ellie, there could be no mistaking what she felt for her.

Ellie handed the drawing back to Den. "Maybe she's hanging on to that idea because it's a safe option."

"What do you mean?"

"I'm not available. There's no danger that I'm going to invade her space, disrupt her carefully ordered life."

"Is that what I'm doing?"

"In a way, I suppose. Probably explains the mixed messages."

Den folded the paper and put it back in her pocket. "Well, I'm certainly confused."

"Give it time. It'll work out." Ellie stood up. "I'm heading over to the studio, hon."

Robin wanted to gather her in her arms to dispel the images of her with Kathryn in her head. "Okay. I thought we might take a walk along the canal. There are some interesting boats moored up for the festival. And Jo might be in."

"Good idea. Catch you later." Ellie kissed her chastely on the cheek and walked over to the door.

Robin watched her pocket one of the flat keys and leave before turning to face Den. "So, are you up for a walk?"

"Sure, it was a long drive. I could do with stretching my legs. Oh, hang on, I just need to text Henry to let him know the car's okay." She got her phone out and started a message.

"Where are you parked?"

"A side street somewhere."

"We'll go and get it. There's parking spaces at the back."

It didn't take them long to locate the car and drive it over to the residents' car park behind the building.

"Thanks," said Den. "I feel better about it being here."

"Not to mention saving on parking fees. The traffic wardens are pretty fierce around here."

They walked across the road, through a small park and over a bridge to the canal towpath. The warm weather was bringing everyone out—walkers, joggers, cyclists—and narrow boats were lining up to get through the locks.

"Do you remember Jo Bright Flame?" Robin asked when they had made it past the marina.

"Is she the one with a dog?"

"That's right. Harry."

"Well, vaguely. I must have met her at your wedding. Bushy brown hair, quite long, and wearing large hoop earrings which I seem to recall she told me were made from recycled toilet rolls or something."

"I doubt it was toilet rolls, but that's Jo. She makes a lot of stuff from things other people discard and sells it. And now she's living on a boat along here. She calls it a craft barge. Making a killing with sock puppets lately."

"Sock puppets. You're having me on."

"No. Really. Some of them are amazing. And she's just got into producing loom bands and can't sell them fast enough."

Den stopped suddenly. "Hey, you're not trying to set me up with her are you?"

"Fuck, no. She's got a girlfriend anyway. Nah, she's a good mate and she saved me from making an arse of myself last night."

"You mean when Kathryn turned up?"

Robin narrowed her eyes at her. "How did you know that?"

"Easy. You always look like you're going to explode whenever her name is mentioned. Sorry."

"No, I mean, how did you know she was here last night?"

"Kieran told me when I stopped in at the farm. What was she doing at the gallery, Robin?"

"I wish I knew. She said she was 'just looking'. But I don't know if she meant the paintings or Ellie. She didn't stay long once Dr Ed and Kieran showed up." Robin stopped by a colourfully painted boat. Flowers and herbs in pots lined the top of the cabin. She tapped on one of the round windows and instantly an enthusiastic bark greeted her.

The door in the well was open and a furry black-and-white bundle hurtled out. Paws on the railing the dog barked at the intruders on the bank.

"Hey, Harry, calm down. It's only me." She reached down and he sniffed her hand before giving it a lick.

Jo's head poked out of the doorway. "Robin! Come on in."

Robin made the introductions and Harry sniffed at Den before she was able to sit down in the cramped interior of the boat. Jo swept aside some materials that were cluttering up the bench seat and the table to make room for Robin to sit as well. While she made tea she asked if Den had come to see Ellie's artwork. Den just nodded. Robin wasn't prepared for the next question when Jo asked innocently, "It was good of Dr Moss to come over for the open evening, wasn't it?"

"Yeah, it was sort of on her way to Durham," Robin couldn't help saying sarcastically.

"Oh, what's she doing in Durham?"

Robin looked over at Den to see if she was okay with the line of questioning. Den just shrugged and told Jo about the professor's new job. She elaborated, telling her about the trip to Dorset and wondering if she could clock up archaeological miles, like air miles. Robin was glad she had lightened the tone.

Jo handed round mugs of something that looked and smelled like canal water. "What's this?" asked Robin.

"Chamomile. It's very relaxing." Jo gave them both a penetrating look. "You look like that's what you need."

Robin shook her head. She was used to Jo's pronouncements but wasn't sure what Den would make of them. Hopefully, Jo wouldn't bring out her crystals. However her next statement was just as off the wall.

"You know, Den, you might have something there. About archaeological miles. I mean it could be there is a ley line that's drawing you and Kathryn towards Durham. An energy force from Stonehenge through Starling Hill to Durham. I would think that's pretty much a straight line."

"Jesus, Jo. Even for you that's a crazy idea."

"Don't mock, Robin. Just because you can't see it, doesn't mean it's not there."

"Okay. But do you have any regular tea, because I don't think I can drink this?"

Jo tutted at her and got up to put the kettle on again. Robin moved the conversation on to the cycle race and Jo's plans for the next day. Den was looking pensive and didn't join in. When Jo suggested she take Harry for a walk, Robin just nodded and called to the dog, who was dozing on the deck.

†

Much as she tried, Kathryn couldn't get the images of both Ellie and her artwork out of her head. She would have to find a way to get Ellie to sell her the painting. It would complement the display being prepared at the British Museum. Kathryn could see it being used for the poster advertising campaign. Ellie had captured the essence of the two lovers as she had imagined them—Cazza and Vee, her nicknames for Cartimandua and Vellocatus.

Joining the slow crawl up the A1 Kathryn debated whether or not to stop at the Scotch Corner services. However, noting the stream of cars ahead signalling to turn off she decided to carry on. It was only another forty minutes to Durham. The air-con in the car was keeping her cool and she wanted to have time to check out the area around the apartment building before meeting the estate agent. Having researched it on Google Maps she had noted that it was within walking distance of the university. However, that could mean a heavy student population.

Driving into Durham she was reminded again of how small it was. The castle and the cathedral dominated the landscape while the university campus seemed to encroach on half the town. She found a parking space near the apartment and walked by the building to view it from the outside. The exterior looked well kept and she noted the private parking area with satisfaction. The surrounding streets seemed quiet even though it was very close to the town centre. And, much to her delight, there was a small café just around the corner that looked to be a comfortable haven. She went in, ordered a latte and made her way to the toilets. Also clean and bright. So far, the city was making her feel welcome.

Refreshed after the coffee and a homemade scone, she walked back to the apartment to meet the agent. The young man with the clipboard who emerged from the front of the building to greet her looked about twelve. He led her up a wide staircase to the second floor and opened the door to the flat. It was lighter inside than she expected and it seemed larger as well. And the views of the river were stunning. The three bedrooms meant she could use one as her study. If Den should decide to join her, she could have her own space as well.

The youngster explained that the building was only ten years old, which was why it looked so modern and why two of the bedrooms had en-suite bathrooms. She loved the clean look of the rooms. Comparing the cost with prices in West Yorkshire, she had decided it was affordable especially if she decided to sell the house in Lindley. She didn't think she would see anything else that so closely matched what she wanted, so near to the university. Being able to walk to work would be an added bonus.

Agreeing to make an offer, she went with the young man to his office, only a five-minute walk away in the city centre. He pointed out places of interest to her as they walked. Suddenly the idea of moving didn't seem so daunting. She just needed to give herself time to adjust.

Once she signed all the paperwork she thanked the boy and walked back to her car enjoying the sunshine. The sights and sounds of the new place gave her a growing confidence that she'd made the right decision.

✝

Den found herself looking into Jo's sympathetic brown eyes. When Robin left with Harry, Jo had made another cup of the tea that smelled like rotting weeds. The gentle motion of the boat, the sound of walkers on the towpath, a view of passing feet through the round window made her feel like she was in a time capsule suspended in space and time.

After what seemed like a year of silence, Den finally found her voice. "You saw Kathryn at the gallery. Rob said you stopped her from lashing out."

The other woman took another eternity to answer. She sipped at her tea before saying, "I get how she feels about Kathryn. But there really is nothing for her to worry about. Ellie's totally committed to Robin. If Kathryn thinks there's any chance of a reunion with Ellie, she's deluding herself."

"So, am I being an idiot then? Chasing after someone whose heart is somewhere else?"

Another narrow boat passed and the slap of water against the side along with an increased rocking motion made Den feel faintly sick. On the other hand it could have been the close confines of the boat's interior with the combined smells of dog, patchouli oil, and chamomile tea.

Jo gave her another one of her inscrutable looks. "I don't think you're an idiot. I feel there is something there. You're on a path. It looks impassable now but you will get there. The vibes are right. You're a Taurus, aren't you?"

"I suppose I am. My birthday is in May."

"And Kathryn's what? Let me think. I would say she's a Virgo. Which means you two are perfectly compatible."

"Sorry, Jo. I don't mean to be rude. But I don't really believe in any of that stuff."

"Just because you don't believe, doesn't mean it's not true."

Den took as deep a breath as she dared and sniffed at the tea. It didn't smell any better but she took a mouthful. She wished she'd asked for some ordinary tea, as Robin had. She wished she had gone with her to take the dog for a walk. Instead she was listening to Jo's pronouncements on her love life, which she thought had all the veracity of a fairground fortuneteller's. She decided to change the subject and hoped Robin would return soon.

"About these ley lines. Do you really believe in them?"

Jo was only too happy to tell her what she knew about the lines of power crisscrossing the British Isles. Den thought it made about as much sense as anything she'd ever read about stone circles and the like. However, an idea for an article started to form in her head and by the time Robin returned with Harry she found she had even started to enjoy the taste of the tea.

Relieved to be out in the open air and on the way back to the flat, Den asked Robin, "How did you know Jo wanted to talk to me alone?"

"I can read Jo pretty well. We lived together last year." She caught Den's surprised look. "Oh, not like that. We shared a house here for a few weeks when Ellie and I were having some time apart. She's not as flaky as she sounds, or looks."

Den wasn't sure about that. The woman had some interesting theories on the pathways of the ancient Britons, a pre-Roman world populated with Druids, women warriors, and magic. But she wasn't buying into any star sign bullshit.

†

Jasmine gulped back the tears. This wasn't what she wanted. She couldn't do this. Not even for Max.

"Hey, you okay?"

A woman came out of one of the stalls. In her misery, Jas hadn't realised there was anyone else in the toilets.

"Not really."

The woman walked over to the sink to wash her hands. Jas caught her eyes in the mirror. She finished washing her hands, looked around for the dryer and just stood shaking off the water before heading back into a stall and grabbing some toilet paper.

"I hate those dryer things," she said, tossing the wadded up paper into the bin. "Too much noise and they do a crap job anyway." She was looking closely at Jas. "I know you, don't I? You're Den's friend, Jasmine, right?"

"Um, yes. How do you know Den?" Jas took in the woman's outfit. Tight leather pants, leather vest, and cuffs. Chains and other metal things hanging off her thick leather belt. "She's not into this kind of scene."

"We live in the same house. I don't see much of her but yeah, you're right. She's not into this. I didn't think you were either when I saw you at the birthday bash."

"Oh, so you're Steph."

"Great process of elimination since the other two inhabitants are men." Steph looked her over again. "So, you're obviously not okay. What are doing crying in the toilets?"

"I just…I can't do what she wants me to do."

"Ah. She being one Max Fleetwood. Well, if you want to do a runner, you better do it quick. She'll be sending someone to look for you if you're in here too long."

"I thought it was just a bit of fun." Jas started crying again.

"Okay. Look, I'll get you out of here. There's a back way. But we'll take this off first." Steph stepped up next to her and unclipped her collar. "I'll leave it on the sink. She'll know what it means. Now stick close behind me and don't look round."

Although following Steph might be jumping from the frying pan into the fire, Jasmine knew there wasn't really any choice. If she were going to get out of this situation, she would have to do it.

✝

Steph looked down at the sleeping woman wondering how she could fall asleep so easily. She was still wired from the events of the night and would need some time to wind down.

The drop from the fire escape hadn't been more than six feet. She had let herself down first then talked Jasmine over the railing and held on to her legs until the woman had been able to drop down beside her. It was fortunate she had brought her van this evening and had parked down a side street so they were able to get to it without going past the front of the club.

As soon as they arrived at Jasmine's flat her mobile phone rang. "It's her," she said.

Of course, thought Steph. *She's the type who would have a different ring tone for friends and family.* "You'll need to block her number. Does Max have your home number?"

"No. She usually calls me at work or on the mobile."

"Does she know where you live?"

"I don't think so."

"But she could find out. She has a lot of contacts."

"Yes." Jasmine looked to be on the verge of tears again as she fumbled in her pocket for her door key.

Steph took a few minutes to think about the situation while the woman opened the door and went in. She followed her into the hallway. "I don't think you should stay here. I can take you back to my place. Den's away so you could stay in her room. She's your mate so I don't suppose she'll mind."

Jasmine had just nodded. She seemed to be in a state of shock. Steph had to take charge and picked out some clothes and collected toiletries from the bathroom. She'd asked if she needed anything else, any medication. A shake of the head was all she got in reply.

It was gone midnight when they arrived at the house. Steph was used to coming home when everyone else was in bed. She managed to get Jasmine up the stairs to Den's room, half carrying her. A bit on the heavy side, she thought, but the rounded curves of her body were easy on the eye. *Steady on, hot stuff, she doesn't need you lusting after her.*

Undressing the unresisting woman had been easy. Ms Fleetwood had obviously selected the outfit for quick removal. Once free from the clothing, Jasmine sighed once, rolled over and went to sleep.

Steph watched the rise and fall of her breasts and took in a deep breath. No, it wasn't going to be easy getting to sleep tonight.

†

From Ellie's point of view, the weekend had been perfect. Apart from the brief encounter with Kathryn on Friday at the open evening, everything had gone well. The gallery had attracted more visitors than usual and all the paintings sold, except one. Helen had begged her to reconsider. She said there had been more offers for that one painting than any of the others. But she wasn't ready to part with it yet.

To complete her happiness, Aiden and Sophie had come over on the train Sunday with baby Wren. Being a grandmother wasn't as awful as she had thought when she first found out Sophie was expecting. She absolutely doted on her granddaughter. And her son's transition into responsible fatherhood had surprised her further. She had feared he would never grow out of adolescence, even at the age of thirty-four.

The carnival atmosphere on the day was intoxicating with warm sunny weather thrown in as a bonus. Den had wandered over to the park during the morning and reported back on the huge numbers gathering, not just there but along the streets as well. Robin made sure their fridge was well stocked with beers and white wine and they had a cupboard full of snacks. The shouts from the crowds below drew them out onto the balcony. But it was just the sponsors' vehicles throwing out goodies to the spectators. Robin turned on the television to find out where the riders were. They were still in Haworth and had the whole of Oxenhope Moor to cross before coming down past them on the way through the town. Helicopters overhead warned the watchers that the frontrunners were close. The scenes of the great crowds across the moor were stunning. People had camped out overnight to be certain of getting a roadside view. It looked perilous for the cyclists with the moving masses so close.

"They're showing Heptonstall church now," Robin yelled from the living room.

"But they're not going through Heptonstall," said Ellie.

"Probably just want to get in a mention of Sylvia Plath." Den knew from her English coursework that visiting the American poet's grave in the churchyard of the nearby hilltop village was still a pilgrimage for her many fans.

"Okay. They're on their way down the hill now," cried Robin. "Oh, fuck! Can you believe it? Sodding ads." She came out on the balcony. "It won't take them long to get down here."

"Sit down, love." Ellie patted the seat next to her. She hadn't expected to feel much excitement about the race, but the festival atmosphere surrounding them was intoxicating.

The first dozen riders flew past in a blur of motion as everyone cheered them on. The peloton arrived in their wake a few minutes later.

"Wouldn't you just give up if you were stuck in the middle of that lot?" asked Aiden as they watched the large group pedal by.

"You'd think so but they're all timed from when they start, so even if you're at the back you're not going to be far off the time of the riders at the front, but obviously the ones that have broken away from the pack are going to have an advantage."

"I didn't think you were that interesting in cycling, Rob."

"It's been all over the papers here for months. Couldn't avoid it. This is like having the Olympic Games or World Cup football in Yorkshire."

There was a long line of support vehicles following the riders and the crowd below started to disperse. Robin and Aiden went inside to watch the next section of the race on TV.

"Look, Ellie, thanks for everything. I thought I would set off up to Durham," Den said.

"They're not reopening the roads until this evening. You might as well stay the night. And, anyway, Helen's invited us over for a barbecue."

"What, all of us?" asked Sophie.

"Yes. It's such a lovely day, we'll be able to lounge around in the garden."

The baby, who had slept through all the noise of the race, woke up then and yelled at the top of her lungs.

"Well, someone's hungry already." Ellie held out her arms. "I'll take her, Soph, while you get her bottle ready." She rocked Wren while waiting for Sophie to warm the milk and kept a watchful eye on Den who still seemed to be struggling with her emotions. She hoped the barbecue on a warm summer's evening would help dispel the journalist's anxiety. Undoubtedly she wanted to be on her way, to be doing something, but with the roads closed, there was nothing she could do for now.

†

Kathryn sat down on the ancient stone wall and viewed her surroundings with the sense of awe the Northumbrian landscape always gave her—the overwhelming sense of history. The legions stationed here were mostly from the part of Gaul now known as Belgium. They were called Tungrians, although the Romans also called them Gemani. The builders of the wall hadn't all been olive-skinned southerners from Italy, they had been a mix of northern Europeans, well adjusted to the colder climate and damp, bone-chilling weather.

She had walked up the hill from the car park and come to the North Gate to look over the wall to the land beyond. The Picts, thought to be a savage people by the Roman conquerors, populated that wild land. Looking at the fierceness of the landscape it was a wonder that they thought they needed to build a wall to keep the unruly tribes penned in. This largely excavated fort in the middle section of Hadrian's Wall now went by the mundane name of Housesteads. The Romans had called it Vercovicium, a name she preferred.

Deciding to use her free Sunday for a busman's holiday, she had made the hour-long journey from her hotel to visit some of her favourite archaeological sites. From Vercovicium it was only a mile or so to Vindolanda. The ongoing excavations there were always fascinating as each year they uncovered more artefacts from the second and third centuries and, incredibly, more of the writing tablets that had given historians valuable insights into the everyday lives of the soldiers and their families here on this far-flung frontier of the Roman empire.

Walking amongst the ruins she was reminded of the many Sundays during her childhood spent roaming the moors above Sheffield with her father, often venturing into the Peak District. Her first sight of a stone circle had inflamed her imagination and she was hooked. Luckily her father shared her passion for the early history of the British Isles. She had moved through the ages reading everything she could lay her hands on and finally settled on the Roman period as her favourite. When it came to choosing a future path, it was archaeology that beckoned.

Part Three

Chapter Seven

Field Reports

The weekend had been just the kind of chill-out she needed. Hanging out with Robin and Ellie, their family and friends, it all helped Den put things in perspective. The barbecue at the gallery owner's place had been fun too. At one point in the evening, though, she'd had a serious conversation with Robin. The kind of conversation you have when you've had a few drinks and the world seems a mellower place.

She had commented that she thought Robin and Ellie looked really happy.

"Yeah, well I almost lost her," Robin had said. "Hope things work out for you and Kathryn."

"I'm not sure it will. I don't have a good track record with long-term relationships. And neither does she, from what Ellie's said."

"It's a bit scary, I have to admit."

"Scary?"

"Scared I'll screw up again. Scared she'll stop loving me."

"Looks pretty solid to me."

Robin had squeezed her arm. "Hey, buddy, don't let me put you off. It's worth it. This whole love thing. Scary and

147

exhilarating. Like climbing a mountain. There might be a few anxious moments on the way up, but the view from the top is amazing."

Den had laughed and told her she should take up writing. They rejoined the others in the garden and Den watched with a twinge of envy as Robin went over to Ellie and hugged her from behind.

†

One step at a time, Den thought, as she drove north Monday morning. She had a mountain to climb and the summit didn't seem to get any closer.

It was a relief to get off the A1 when she turned to head for the nearest town to the dig site, Bishop Auckland. There was nothing in the town that tempted her to stop. Ever thoughtful, Ellie had got up early and sent her off with a large thermos mug of coffee and a packed lunch. Finding the site was easier than she expected and she was there before she knew it. She sat in the car and sipped the still warm coffee considering her next move. There was no sign of Kathryn's car, but then she may have come with a colleague.

The Romans had called the fort Vinovia, now rendered into English as Binchester. The excavation programme included not just field training for undergraduate students from Durham University but also, she had been surprised to learn, Stanford University in California. And, during July, they invited members of the public to participate by volunteering. The car park was starting to fill up. People were dressed for the weather in shorts and T-shirts. One couple had stopped to slather sunscreen on each other. They were all wearing hats.

She finished her coffee and got out of the car. Catching up to the sunscreen couple she asked them who was in charge. They didn't seem surprised to be accosted by a stranger and just smiled. The man said to follow them. It was almost time for their morning briefing.

Den stood at the back, observing the group. They were a mix of ages and nationalities brought together by a shared enthusiasm for digging around in the dirt to ferret out the secrets of the past. The supervisor, obviously a university lecturer by the way he spoke, told them where they would be working and what they hoped to find. One crew was sent off to trench one and another to trench two. She thought the trench two lot looked a bit more enthusiastic than the others. It seemed they were uncovering floor surfaces in front of a bathhouse. Trench one was a barracks area and consisted of a lot of randomly placed stones. As the crews moved off to collect their tools, Den approached the organiser.

"I didn't think you were one of the regular volunteers," he said after she had introduced herself.

"No. I was told I could find Professor Moss here."

"Professor Moss? Oh, yes, she will be joining us later today. But this morning she's having a tour of the castle, part of her induction." He took in her look of disappointment. "You're welcome to join us while you wait. I can fix you up with a trowel and a bucket."

Den hesitated. But then she thought, why not? She would only spend the time moping around wondering what she was going to say to Kathryn when she saw her. "Okay. But I've never done this before."

"That's fine. I'll put you with one of our more experienced students." They had been walking towards the excavators gathered around the tool shed while they talked. "Jessica!" he called out as soon as they were close. A girl with long brown hair tied back in a ponytail looked up. He waved her over. "We have an extra volunteer today. Would you mind showing her the ropes? She can work with you on your section."

Jessica smiled at him, eager to please. "Yes, of course, Professor."

"Good. I'll come and check up on you in a bit." He walked off to speak to someone else.

The student looked at her. "Your first time?"

"Yes. I'm Den, by the way."

"Okay. Hold on to these and I'll get another set for you." Jessica handed her a bucket and went back to the shed.

Den looked at the kneeling pad, trowel and brush inside the bucket and wondered if she could really do this. Some of the workers were already in position, kneeling on their pads, scraping away at the dirt. How long did they have to work until they got a break? She found it hard to believe they were all volunteers. It looked more like some community payback scheme.

Jessica returned with another bucket. "This way," she said brightly. "We're in trench two. I found a calf's skull last week."

"I thought it was a bathhouse."

"Well, we're just starting to get down to the fourth century level. It was used for something else after the Romans left."

They settled down on their mats and Jessica showed Den how to use the trowel. The bucket was for the excess dirt and the small stones that weren't important. "When you've got as much in your bucket as you can carry, you empty it into the wheelbarrow. And when that's full, take it over to the spoil heap."

"Right. And when do we get a break?"

"We stop for lunch at twelve thirty."

"Oh." Den reckoned that was about two and half hours away. She could only hope Kathryn would show up well before as she wasn't sure how much kneeling her knees could take.

†

Jasmine woke up Saturday morning without the slightest idea where she was. Someone had placed a glass of water by the bed and she drank this gratefully. Looking around she saw a case by the door that looked familiar. Slowly, pieces of information from the night before filtered through.

The flight from the club. Coming here with the strange woman, Steph. Sleeping in Den's room and Den wasn't here.

She drifted in and out of consciousness. The door opening brought her eyes open again.

"You awake?" The voice sounded familiar but she didn't recognise the speaker.

"Yeah, sort of." She sat up, clutching the duvet to her chest.

"You went out like a light last night. All the excitement, I guess."

Jas finally realised it was Steph. Only now she was wearing a loose tank top and running shorts, she didn't look anything like the leather-clad creature of the night. All the bare body parts on display were tanned and Jas remembered that she was a gardener. And she had strength in her arms. Jas flushed at the memory of her legs being held securely while she gathered the courage to drop to the ground from the fire escape.

"I've brought you a cup of tea. Hope you like it with milk. I didn't put any sugar in though."

"That's perfect. Thanks." Jas took the cup from her gratefully.

"Um. Your clothes and stuff...they're in the case. We were in a bit of a hurry last night so hopefully you've got everything you need. There's toothpaste and shampoo in the bathroom at the bottom of the stairs. Just help yourself. Oh, yeah, and the towels are in the airing cupboard in the hall-way."

"Are you saying I look like shit?" Jas ventured a smile.

"Not at all. Just thought you might want a shower." Steph's hair had fallen over her eyes and Jas couldn't tell if she was looking at her or the floor.

"Thanks. That would be great."

"Okay. Well, when you're ready, come on down. I'll be in the garden at the back." Steph gave her a wave and left.

Jas listened to the footsteps going down the stairs then decided it was time to make a move.

The shower felt wonderful. There wasn't a lot of choice from the clothes Steph had selected from her wardrobe. But the sweatpants and T-shirt felt comfortable. With what she had been wearing at the club, Steph would probably think anything was an improvement. She saw the offending items on the floor by the bed and shivered. This woman she hardly knew had also undressed her last night. So first impressions couldn't possibly be any worse.

Jas found her way down to the kitchen and saw the open doors to the garden. Steph was bending over a flowerbed examining the leaves of a plant.

"Hi," she said, feeling suddenly shy.

Steph straightened up. "Ah. Good. Have a seat. I'll make you something to eat." She brushed her unruly fringe off her face with the back of one grubby hand.

"I don't want to put you to any trouble."

"No worries. Henry's the gourmet cook around here. Cheese sandwiches are my specialty."

"Where are the guys?"

"They went off to meet some friends in town."

Sitting out in the small garden had a calming effect on her nerves. But as she started to remember why she was here and not at home, anxiety set in again. She nibbled at the sandwich Steph brought her. The woman seemed to sense her unease and went back into the house, reappearing moments later with two glasses of chilled white wine.

"This should hit the spot," she said, sitting down and taking a large sip from her own glass.

"Yes. Thank you." It was close enough to midday for it to feel okay to be drinking wine for breakfast. Like she was on holiday, sitting on a patio in the sun talking to someone she'd just met.

Steph stared out at the garden for a few minutes. Finally she asked, "Do you want to tell me about it?"

"About what?"

"About what Max Fleetwood wanted you to do?"

"Oh, that." Jasmine bit into the sandwich and chewed slowly, giving herself time to think. "At first I thought she was suggesting a threesome. You know, with another woman. I think I could have handled that, maybe. But then I found out she was loaning me to someone else. A man." Jas gulped her wine, unable to look at Steph.

"Jesus! I knew she was heavy-duty, but really, a man?"

Jasmine just nodded, miserably.

"Okay. Well, I guess I understand why you wanted out."

"Do you think I'm stupid...for getting involved with her?"

Steph took her time to answer, finishing her drink in one quick swig. She swallowed before turning to Jas. "No. If you've not been around the scene you wouldn't know about her reputation. But then, when I saw you here at that party, I wouldn't have pegged you for one of the vulnerable types who usually fall for her."

"Well, I wouldn't have thought of myself that way either. I suppose though, at least, going with her I finally got Robin out of my system."

"Who's Robin?"

"A woman from up north. I thought she was the one, you know. But there was someone else and they're married now."

"Hey, that sucks. I'm sorry." Steph got up and went into the house. She came out with the bottle and filled Jas's glass and then her own.

They sat in silence for a time, sipping their wine. Steph got up to deadhead one of the roses. Jas admired the view of her strong legs disappearing into the skimpy shorts and the outline of a firm butt as she bent over the plant. This was someone who worked out seriously.

Sitting down again, Steph brushed her hair aside again and looked over at Jas. "How did you meet Max Fleetwood? If you don't mind talking about it."

"Through work. She's a client. Quite an important one."

"Hard to say no to her then?"

"Yes." To her surprise, Jas found herself on the verge of tears.

"I'm sorry. I shouldn't have brought it up."

"No, it's okay. I...just...I don't know how I let it happen. Last night. I mean, I knew before I got to the club that something strange was going on. That outfit, for a start. I feel like such a fool." The tears were streaming now.

"Hey, look." Steph took one of her hands and started stroking it gently. "Don't get down on yourself. You had the sense to know when to get out."

Jas nodded. She liked the feel of Steph's strong fingers on her hand and they sat like that for several minutes as she felt herself calm down. Steph got up again and fetched a tissue for her. She blew her nose and finished the wine.

When she had recovered her composure, Steph suggested they go for a walk by the river and told her they would need the exercise because Henry was cooking his famous coq au vin for dinner.

†

The director of excavations had offered to show her around the castle on Monday morning before going out to the dig site, and when she accepted Kathryn hadn't expected the tour to last more than half an hour. However, he seemed keen to elaborate on every aspect of the castle's features, nine hundred years of history. And the university had occupied the castle for a hundred and eighty-two of those years.

Kathryn was sure she could have gleaned the information more quickly from a tourist guidebook. He had then insisted on taking her down the hill to the Old Fulling Mill by the river. Until that month, this former corn mill had been the site of the university's Museum of Archaeology. The artefacts were in the process of being boxed up to be transported to their new premises in the Palace Green Library, a much more accessible position between the cathedral and the castle. Kathryn barely managed to rein in her impatience. However, she was going to have to work with the man, so she just smiled and agreed to the additional tour.

By the time they reached the site it was going on half past twelve and Kathryn was ready to strangle her new colleague. They had driven over in her car as he said he would be getting a lift back with his number two, who was already on site. It was fortunate he had been free that morning, he'd told her. If they'd had a school group in he wouldn't have been able to be on hand to show her round. She forced another smile.

"Looks like they're just stopping for lunch," he said as they approached the excavation area.

Kathryn's experienced gaze swept over the neatly placed rows of wheelbarrows and she complimented him on what looked like a well-run dig.

"Well, it is mostly a training exercise for the undergrads. Make sure they're up to scratch. And it helps to give the visitors a good impression."

"Of course," she murmured.

"Have you got something to eat? I'm sorry, I should have checked before we left the campus."

"Yes. The hotel provided a packed lunch." Kathryn had collected her backpack from the boot of the car before they left the car park.

"Right. Well, I'll introduce you to Norm and we'll find out what's been happening this morning."

They made their way over to the shed where the group of volunteers was gathered. Some seated in groups outside eating their sandwiches and chatting while others were inside, making tea or coffee.

Kathryn stopped and stared. It couldn't be. She would know that shaggy crop anywhere. Den was sitting talking to a young woman with a ponytail. She seemed immersed in the conversation.

"Would you like to talk to the excavators, Kathryn? Or do you want to join myself and Norm?"

"Um. Yes, sorry. I'll join you." Kathryn followed him to a seating area behind the hut. She was still in shock and didn't take in much of what the two men were talking about. *Damn you, Den. Couldn't you have just phoned?* She didn't know how she was going to handle the situation. This was far too public for having any kind of emotional scene and in front of her new colleagues as well.

†

Den closed the lid of the laptop with a sigh and glanced around again. It had gone five and no sign of Kathryn yet. Jessica had told her the finishing time at the dig was four or four thirty but sometimes the archaeologists hung around longer, examining the finds of the day and working out which areas needed more attention. The student had been a good interviewee as Den found herself unconsciously going into interview mode when talking with her. Without revealing anything about herself, she had discovered quite a bit about the girl's ambitions, what she thought of the course and her tutors. Jessica had been enthusiastic about the addition of Dr Moss to the faculty. Everyone was talking about it. She was something of a celebrity in their world.

The bar was empty and she'd been nursing the pint of lager for an hour. Even the barman had disappeared. Probably nattering with the kitchen crew. Checking her phone again, there was nothing since the brief text from Kathryn just giving her the name of the hotel and the time she expected to be there. Den had exhausted her interest in the new game Robin had introduced to her. Just as she was thinking the whole trip was turning into an epic fail, Kathryn walked in. Her appearance wasn't the groomed look she normally sported. A hastily removed hat gave her hair more of a bed-head look, one that Den would have liked to be responsible for.

"Come up to my room," she said curtly. "We can't talk in here." And without giving Den more than a cursory glance, she turned on her heel and walked out.

Den grabbed her bag, stuffing the laptop in, and quickly walked to catch up with her as she reached the stairs. She stayed a few steps behind, trying to read her mood from the back.

Once inside the room, Kathryn strode over to the window and looked out. Den stood on the far side of the bed, suddenly unsure of her reception.

"Why didn't you let me know you were coming?" Kathryn didn't turn around as she spoke.

"I don't know. I thought you'd be pleased to see me."

"I would if you hadn't turned up my first day on the job. I could barely concentrate on my work."

"Oh, so my presence does have some effect on you." Den felt her temper rising.

Kathryn didn't say anything. She was standing by the window staring out, arms crossed.

"Because I don't really know what you think of our so-called relationship." Den fished out the now much crumpled drawing and threw it on the bed. "What was this supposed to mean? I get a short note saying you think we can work something out long distance over time and a drawing that would make the mother of a five-year-old proud. I was tempted to put it up on the fridge door. Then I come up north thinking it might be a good idea to spend some time together, your suggestion if you recall, and find out that you've been sniffing around Ellie again." Den couldn't help the anger and frustration now seeping into her tone.

"I wasn't...sniffing. I went to the gallery to see her paintings."

"Yeah, right."

"Yes, right. I saw an ad in the paper about the open evening and wanted to see what her work was like. I just thought she was dabbling in it, something to while away long winter evenings. I was surprised at how good they were. Not just paint-by-numbers." Animated now, the professor continued, oblivious to Den's upset. "And I was completely blown away by the one she's done of Starling Hill with Cazza and Vee. Did you see it? I have to convince her to sell it to me."

Den looked at her, exasperated. "Kathryn! You're avoiding the issue...again."

"What do you want me to say?"

"Maybe start with an indication that you want me to be here. Maybe move on to you want to be with me. I'm getting the feeling that you don't want either."

"You brought Ellie up."

"Yes, well. It's always Ellie, isn't it? It's always going to be Ellie." Den picked up her bag. "This was a waste of time. I should have known." She looked back when she reached the door. Kathryn was still standing by the window staring out. "Goodbye." She resisted slamming the door behind her.

Den sat in Henry's car, head on her arms on the steering wheel. Crying was a waste of time as well she thought. She'd done enough of that. She was bone-tired after spending the day digging and her wrists were sore. It wouldn't be a good idea to drive anywhere. After a few more minutes considering her options, she looked out at the hotel. Might as well see if they had any rooms available.

†

Jas knew she still looked like crap. Her eyes were puffy and Steph hadn't packed any of her makeup in the flight from her flat Friday night. A pale but not very interesting look, she thought.

Monday morning. She needed to think about going to work. A knock on the door and Steph poked her head round cautiously.

"Oh, you're up. Would you like some tea?"

"Not really. A frothy full fat cappuccino would be nice, with chocolate on top."

Steph pushed the door open and came in. She sat on the chair by the desk and gave her a sideways glance from under her fringe. "You're not thinking of going in to work, are you?"

"Well, yes, I was."

"Maybe you should take some time off. Phone in sick."

"Do I really look that bad?"

"Look." Steph flicked the unruly hair out of her eyes with the movement that Jas was starting to find endearing. "Max Fleetwood's a client, right?"

"Yes."

"She's not going to let go that easily. The longer she doesn't know where you are the better."

"Won't it just piss her off more?" Jas thought of all the missed calls on her phone. Max's number had shown up ten times on Sunday, but no message was left. More than likely some other acolyte was told to make the calls.

Steph shrugged. "Nah. By next week she'll have moved on to someone else. I just think you should lay low for a while."

Jas picked at the duvet cover. "Could you phone in for me?" She knew she sounded like a petulant teenager not wanting to go to school and face the bullies.

"Sure. But I better use your phone. She already has that number."

Jas looked up at her, puzzled.

"You know, in case one of your colleagues tries to track you down for her. Which reminds me, we should see about getting you a new SIM card."

"Steph, I don't know how to thank you for doing this. You hardly know me."

The other woman looked embarrassed. "Hey, don't worry about it. It's nothing I wouldn't do for anyone in this situation." She stood up and walked to the door. "I can't promise you a cappuccino. Will a strong coffee do?"

Jas nodded and watched her go. It was true they hardly knew each other but she felt there was a bond developing between them, a growing friendship. During Saturday evening's walk along the river and more long walks on Sunday, they had talked. The only jarring note had come when Jas's mother phoned wanting to know when she was coming for dinner and bringing her fiancé. It seemed she was already making wedding plans for her and Max.

Steph had only heard her side of the conversation but it was enough to make her question Jas on it. So she told Steph about her problem of not having come out to her parents and her mother's expectations to see her happily married before she reached another landmark age, this time fifty. It hadn't been so bad at thirty and forty. Her father, at least, understood her desire to have a career and be independent.

"What about your parents? When did you come out to them?" she had asked Steph.

"I didn't have to. I knew from an early age what I was and they never made a big deal of it. Maybe they thought I would grow out of it. But I was adopted so I guess they could blame it on my genes, which weren't theirs. It wasn't their fault."

"Have you ever wanted to find your birth mother?"

"I tried. I was in my first year at uni and someone told me about the Salvation Army records. He had been able to trace his siblings through them. They'd been split up when their parents died in a traffic accident. But there was nothing on either of my parents. It was like I'd been dropped by aliens."

Jas smiled at this. She'd seen the books in Steph's room, mainly science fiction and fantasy. A strange preference she thought for someone who had studied law at university and then abandoned a lucrative career as a solicitor to take up gardening. She'd told Jas she preferred being outdoors, being her own boss. And, of course, being able to wear what she wanted. She hadn't been able to see herself lasting long in the world of pinstripe suits playing power games in the big city.

†

Standing by the coffee machine, watching the water fil-
ter through, Steph tried to work out what she was feeling.
*The woman's in a vulnerable space. You can't go there even
if you are attracted.*

"Smells good. I didn't think you knew how to use that."

Steph turned and looked at Henry. "You'd be surprised
what I know."

"I'm sure I would. So, how's our guest?"

"She's okay." Steph hadn't told Henry and Paul the
whole story. Just that Jas was recovering from a painful
breakup and needed a bolt hole for a while. They had both
been sympathetic and, as she knew they would, had been
kind to Jas when they'd all had dinner together Saturday
evening.

"Have you heard from Den?" Steph really wanted to
know if the journalist was due back any time soon.

"Not since yesterday. So I'm assuming she's with
Kathryn now."

"I can't believe you let her borrow your car. You'll
probably never see it again. Not in one piece, anyway."

"Actually, she's quite a good driver and I know she
won't take any risks in it."

Jas appeared in the kitchen doorway. Henry smiled at
her and gestured for her to come in and sit down.

"Thanks. The coffee smells great."

"We were just talking about Den. I don't suppose she's
contacted you." Henry was giving Jas a sympathetic look.

"No. But she often goes offline when she's pursuing a
lead."

"We thought she was pursuing the elusive professor."

"Last time we talked things weren't going too well in
that area."

Steph poured out the coffee and sat opposite Jas, trying
not to stare too obviously at the breasts that were threatening

to spill out from the skimpy top she was wearing. She couldn't think of anything to say and was thankful Henry was there to carry on the conversation.

"Well, it seemed to be on track again after they found each other in Dorset."

"Dorset?"

"Yes, I know. It's a long story." Henry waved his arms around. "It's still up in the air. Dr Moss is happy to continue a long-distance relationship but Den is hankering after a home sweet home scenario."

"That's not like the Den I know." Jas sipped her coffee and smiled at Steph. "This is marvellous. Thank you."

Steph felt like her insides would melt. How could this happen in such a short time? She'd only met the woman Friday evening and in dubious circumstances, and now she thought she was in love.

Henry carried on, oblivious, thankfully. "I know. But she's totally besotted. I've never seen her like this."

Den wasn't the only one, thought Steph. *It must be in the air.* The first time she'd seen Jas, at the birthday party in May, there had been no flicker of interest at all. Maybe now it was because she had seen her at her most vulnerable, as well as completely naked. She flushed as the images from Friday night filtered through, undressing the semiconscious woman, watching her fall asleep, and fighting the desire to crawl into the bed with her. Just to hold, to comfort, that's what she had told herself. She wasn't like Max Fleetwood. She knew how to nurture. She knew that the games she enjoyed could only be played with a partner's complete love and trust. She knew, somehow, that Jas could be that partner.

†

Kathryn stood at her window looking out, seeing nothing. When had she turned into such a coward? Seeing Den at the site had been a shock but any normal human being would have immediately gone over and said something. They could have talked. Found somewhere private. Perhaps then, Den's anger wouldn't have built up as it obviously had.

She didn't know how long she'd stood there before making up her mind to go after the journalist. Grabbing the door key, she ran down the stairs and out the front door. The car park was at the side of the building. There was no sign of the old banger Den had been using in Dorset. None of the cars parked looked like anything Den would drive. Certainly not the almost new, white BMW. She was positive a car like that surely belonged to a sales rep of a multinational company who would be overnighting in the hotel.

Back in her room she picked up her phone. Just call her, the rational voice in her head said. The emotional one took over and voiced doubts about what to say. Den was right to be upset about her visit to the gallery. She hadn't just wanted to see the paintings. She was still lusting after the artist. Lusting. That was too strong a word. She was a professional, a professor of archaeology who lectured hundreds of students with confidence, wrote highly respected academic papers, spoke at conferences to scores of her peers. Surely she could handle one volatile journalist.

She rang Den's number. After ten rings it went onto voice mail. She cancelled it. Finally, on the third attempt she managed to leave a message. She sat on the bed not sure what she wanted most, a shower and change of clothes, or a drink, or both at once.

The phone rang just as she made it to the bathroom door. She lunged at it and knocked her knee on the edge of the bed. It wasn't Den, though. The number wasn't one she recognised. Hoping it was one of her new colleagues and not a random sales call, she answered.

†

The bed was comfortable and after her day of unaccustomed activity, Den fell asleep as soon as she lay down. When she woke it was dark outside and she was surprised to see it was ten o'clock. She rang room service and ordered a chicken sandwich and a beer. The best they could offer was Newcastle Brown. No surprise she thought, considering the proximity to that city.

She had just finished in the shower and donned the hotel bathrobe when the knock on the door came. She opened it and stood aside to let the waiter deliver the order. When he'd gone, she sat down at the table and devoured half a sandwich, and drank most of the beer in several large gulps. Leaving the rest of the sandwich, she lay back on the bed and turned the television on to watch the news, falling asleep again before they got to the weather forecast.

Den woke up and checked the time on the clock by the bed. Seven. It had been a long time since she'd slept a full eight hours. And that wasn't counting the hours she'd slept after booking into the room. She rolled over and groped around for her phone. There were several missed calls. All from Kathryn. She sat up and looked at the phone again. Why hadn't she heard it? Then she remembered, she'd put it on silent while she was at the dig.

Only one of the calls had a message. The sound of Kathryn's voice brought the emotions of the day before charging back. Sounding contrite, tearful almost, she wanted to talk.

Den went to the bathroom to wash and dress. Then she sat down on the bed to listen to the message again. Although it was still early, she thought Kathryn would be awake. Her room was only a few doors away, so it wouldn't hurt to call her back and see what she had to say for herself.

No answer. It went straight to voice mail. Den decided not to leave a message. She would find her at the dig.

The hotel breakfast provided far more calories than Den would normally ingest at that time of day. One cup of tepid coffee, however, convinced her she would need to find a decent coffee shop before going to the site. She checked out of the hotel. Depending on the outcome of her conversation with Kathryn she would either be coming back to share her bed or going back to London.

She walked out onto the street and around the corner and immediately found what she was looking for—a café with a gourmet deli. Ordering a double shot espresso, she also bought a baguette filled with hummus and chargrilled vegetables to take away. She downed the coffee while waiting for the sandwich and decided to take a cappuccino with her as well. The site was in the middle of nowhere and it would be as well to be prepared today. And if she ended up going home, it would save her having to eat some crap at a motorway services.

Back in the car she tried Kathryn's phone again. Still no answer.

Two coaches were taking up space in the car park when she arrived at the fort. She eventually found a space she could manage to get the BMW into without endangering the paintwork. Maneuvering with care as she opened the door, she was just able to squeeze through the narrow gap without touching the next vehicle. She wandered over to the reception area and hoped they would remember that she had been part of the dig crew the day before. Although today she wasn't really dressed for it, having reverted to wearing jeans.

Luckily she saw Jessica just ahead and called out to her. The girl turned and waited for her to catch up.

"Hi. Are you back for more?"

"I don't think I'm really cut out for it. But I enjoyed yesterday."

"It should be fun today. I've been asked to help out with the school tour."

That explained the presence of the coaches.

"Oh, good." Den smiled at the girl. "That will give you a break from being on your knees all day. Have you seen Professor Moss this morning?"

"No. She won't be around today. Her father's been taken ill over at Blackpool. I heard one of the other professors saying she got a call last night. A heart attack, I think."

"Really." No wonder she wasn't answering her phone. Den bit her lip. "Look, I've got something I need to do today. Hope you enjoy doing the tour guide bit. Catch you later." She walked briskly back to her car and once inside stared out of the windscreen. Ellie had said Kathryn was close to her father. The only time the professor had mentioned her parents to her, she'd said they were both super fit, always playing golf, and lived by the sea. She didn't think it was Blackpool, though. Probably the closest hospital with a cardiac unit. Doing the maths, Den realised Kathryn's parents would have to be in their seventies, possibly eighties.

Breathing deeply, she told herself to get on with it. She switched on the ignition and entered Blackpool into the satnav. It thought about it for some time and once it had figured out where she was, informed her the journey would take two hours without traffic. She figured two and a half was more likely.

The further north you were in England, the fewer cross-country options you had and it was, she realised, almost coast-to-coast. Well, at least it wasn't Cornwall. That would have taken most of the day. She finished the rest of the cappuccino and backed out of the space. Before joining the main road, she stopped to plug in her phone and put the iPod on shuffle mode. Might as well enjoy some tunes over the next few hours. Singing along to some of her favourites could help her shut out thoughts of what Kathryn might be going through. She rubbed at her shoulder remembering the last time she had seen Kathryn at a hospital. Only that time she was the patient.

Chapter Eight

Translations

The last two days had been wonderful. Jasmine found herself telling Steph things she'd never told anyone, things she had barely admitted to herself. Monday morning, Steph had phoned her office and told Ray she wasn't well, some kind of flu thing. Then she'd suggested that Jas might want to join her on a job.

"I don't know the first thing about gardening."

"Doesn't matter. I'm just doing some planting out on a patio today. I'll show you what to do."

It seemed like a better option than sitting around in a strange house or going for long walks by herself. That first day had been easy, just potting some plants, deadheading roses. The second day was more arduous with Steph doing heavy-duty hedge trimming. Jas made herself useful filling up the garden waste bags. She found all the bending was more of a workout than anything she had ever done in the gym.

Now, after a refreshing bath and the anticipation of a good meal cooked by Henry, she sat on the floor in the living room with a glass of red wine, relaxing between Steph's knees while the gardener massaged her shoulders. Her hands were firm and strong and Jas was moaning with pleasure, the warmth spreading throughout her body.

"I'll do the same for you," she said. "You must be aching all over."

"I am. And I'll take you up on that after dinner."

She had told Steph how much she hated her job. How the realisation had been creeping up on her slowly the last few years. She was realising that she didn't enjoy the way it made her feel. Telling lies, trying to convince people to buy things they didn't need. Selling products or services she didn't believe in. Just talking to Steph made her realise she should make some changes in her life, that it wasn't impossible, and maybe now was the time to do it.

Jas helped Paul wash up after dinner while Steph went up to her room to get ready for the promised massage.

†

"Are you a relative?" The hospital receptionist eyed her suspiciously.

Den took a deep breath. It was England, 2014, after all. "I'm his daughter's partner."

"Okay." The receptionist actually cracked a smile. "Go on up to the cardiac unit. They'll direct you from there."

Relieved, Den followed the signs and found the ward she was looking for without any trouble.

Of the four beds only two were occupied. One man was asleep and the other was sitting up leafing through a magazine. He looked too tanned and healthy to be taking up a hospital bed. She approached cautiously. "Mr Moss?" she asked quietly, so as not to disturb the other patient.

He looked up and surveyed her through his glasses. She could see the resemblance. Kathryn had the same look, particularly when she was in professor mode.

"And who are you? I've had all my tests and I don't need a social worker."

"I'm Denise Sullivan. I thought Kathryn would be here."

"She's gone home to bring me some fresh pyjamas and a few books." He looked her up and down. "Ah. You're the London one."

Den wasn't sure how to respond to that so she just indicated the seat next to the bed. "May I?"

He nodded.

"If you don't mind me saying so, you're looking pretty good."

"I've had a heart attack, but luckily not a fatal one. Seems my arteries are okay. But they're worried about a blood clot on my lungs. So I'm stuck here until they sort out what to do about it."

"Oh, sorry." Den was keeping her voice low.

"You can speak up. He can't hear you. Deaf as a post."

They looked at each other for several more long moments.

"You're not quite what I expected," he said finally. "But, then, I don't suppose I would know what to expect. I've never met any of Kathryn's girlfriends."

"Yeah, well, I guess I'm just one of a long line." The words were out of Den's mouth before she considered the implication of his statement. "You know about…"

"Yes. I mean, she never talked about it. But she's never talked about any kind of relationships no matter how much her mother would press her on the subject of dating and marriage. Fern gave up eventually."

"So, how do you know I'm the 'London one'?" Den decided she had to know.

"I could tell she was unhappy about something when she visited us recently. She told me about you and the other one, the potter. And then she shot off to London in the middle of the night. Very uncharacteristic." He smiled at her.

"Will she be back soon?"

"Um, no. She's coming back about four. Fern had a mixed doubles match this afternoon so Kathryn took her home to collect her car."

"Your wife's going off to play golf while you're in here?"

"Don't look so shocked. I told her to go. After what's happened to me you never know when you'll get to play your last round."

†

It was shortly after noon when she left the hospital and followed Kathryn's father's directions to his house. She pulled up outside the bungalow and smiled at the name on the gatepost—Fernhow. Mr Moss hadn't told her what his first name was, she could now guess it was Howard. *Fern Moss, though. How did she live with that moniker?* A woman nowadays would probably choose to keep her maiden name.

Kathryn's sporty red car was in the driveway. Taking several deep breaths, she got out of the BMW, locked it carefully and walked up the path. The front door opened before she reached it. The professor emerged wearing a dressing gown, her hair wet and hanging limply, carrying a black bin bag. She peered at Den. Without her glasses and immaculately coiffed hairstyle she looked like a vulnerable teenager. Den wanted to sweep her into her arms and kiss her, sans bin bag.

"Den? What are you doing here?"

"I heard about your dad. Thought you might want some support."

"I...well...oh, hell." She shoved the bag at Den. "Put this in the bin. I've just put the coffee on." She disappeared into the house, leaving Den holding the bag.

Having disposed of the rubbish as instructed, Den followed the coffee smell to the kitchen at the back of the house. It opened out into a conservatory laden with plants and comfortably padded chairs. The coffeemaker gurgled its way to a noisy conclusion and Den helped herself to a mug. She could hear the sound of a hair dryer so she knew it would be at least ten minutes before Kathryn would feel her hair was presentable.

The magazines on the table in the conservatory reminded her of a doctor's waiting room. A choice between *Gardener's World* and *Golf Monthly,* she chose the latter. She knew nothing about the game, but the pictures of the featured golf courses made it look enticing. She was reading about a golf complex in Portugal when Kathryn appeared, dressed now in chinos and a Polo shirt looking like she was heading for the golf course herself.

Nursing her cup of coffee she sat down opposite Den. "Sorry. We didn't get much sleep last night, waiting for the test results. I had to have a shower."

"I saw your dad. He's looking pretty good, considering."

"They let you in to see him?"

"Yes. No problem. I said I was your partner."

Kathryn turned her head away and Den couldn't read her expression. "Where did you go last night?"

"I stayed at the hotel."

The professor looked stunned. "I went out to the car park. I didn't see your car."

"I borrowed Henry's. His pride and joy, we call it PJ."

"Oh. Don't tell me. It's a white BMW."

Den nodded.

"I didn't think you'd be driving anything as flashy as that. I thought you'd gone."

Den put her coffee mug down on the table and moved over to Kathryn. She knelt down and took her hands. "Look. I was upset yesterday and I'm sorry I said those things about Ellie. I just…well, if you haven't figured it out by now, I just want to be with you. If you'll let me."

"I don't know why you want to be with me. As you should know by now I'm not very good at this relationship stuff. Maybe I'm too old for this. You don't really want to hook up with a crusty old dyke."

"Kathryn. I wouldn't be here if this wasn't what I wanted. And you're only as old as you feel, as my mother used to say. However, if you feel like an eighteen-year-old, tough, you've got me." Den caught the flicker of a smile. Seizing the moment she leaned in closer and kissed her on the lips. "I'm sorry," she said as they pulled apart for air. "I know you've just dried your hair, but I'm seriously going to mess it up again."

†

Kathryn lay back on the bed in her parents' spare room and looked across at her lover. Den's long limbs were splayed out everywhere and she was snuffling softly in her sleep. A few hours of gentle lovemaking, Den had seemed to sense her need for sensuous touching rather than frantic foreplay. But when she came, the climax had ripped through her like a hurricane and she had immediately fallen into a deep sleep. She wanted to touch Den now, to wake her and make love to her, but there wasn't time.

It was after three and she needed to collect the things her father wanted. Trying not to disturb Den, she crept out of the room, grabbing the robe from the back of the door as she went. Toiletries were easy, book by the bed, slippers, pyjamas, dressing gown, but she couldn't find his reading glasses anywhere. She was still searching when Den came into her parents' bedroom.

"I thought I heard you in here."

"I can't find his glasses."

"He was wearing glasses when I saw him."

"Those are his driving ones. He needs his reading ones."

"Oh, there was a pair in the conservatory, by the magazines."

"Of course. You're wonderful."

"Yeah, I know." Den reached for her.

"I have to go. I said I'd be back by four and I'm going to be late now."

"I'll come with you."

"You don't have to."

Den pulled her into an embrace. "Kathryn, this is what partners do. I'm here for you."

"I need another shower."

"So do I." Den grinned at her.

Kathryn gave her a playful push. "No, you don't! I want to make it to the hospital sometime today."

†

They drove back to Blackpool in Henry's car. Kathryn commented on Henry's generosity and trust in lending such a beautiful machine to Den.

"He knows I value my life and it wouldn't be worth anything if there's so much as a scratch on PJ when I get back."

Kathryn told her about receiving the call the night before and her frantic drive across country. There hadn't been anything she could do when she arrived at the hospital other than comfort her mother who was in shock.

"He's never had a day's illness in his life, nothing serious anyway. The odd cold and occasional back pain."

"Where did it happen?"

"On the golf course. Luckily one of his playing partners was a doctor."

On arrival at the hospital they were informed that Howard Moss had been moved. After a few minutes of searching on the computer and shuffling piles of clipboards the nurse was able to direct them to the right ward. His eyes were closed as they approached the bed and he looked like he was asleep, but his eyelids fluttered and opened fully when they reached him.

"So, have you two kissed and made up?"

"Dad!"

"Looks like you have." He smiled at them.

Kathryn rested the bag she'd brought on the end of the bed. "I think everything you wanted is in here. If not, Mum can bring it later."

"Do you know what happened to my golf clubs?"

"Yes. Andrew had the presence of mind to get your bag and your trolley taken back to the clubhouse. Mum's going to collect them from the pro shop after her round."

"Oh, good. Doc says I'll be let out Friday. I'll be able to play in the monthly medal on Sunday."

"I'm sure the doctor didn't tell you that. You're going to need to take it easy for a bit."

"But if I have a buggy…"

"Dad! That's not even up for discussion. Phil's coming up Saturday and I'll leave him instructions to tie you to the bed."

Kathryn had never thought she would see the day when she was going to have to be a parent to her parents. They had always been so independent and in control of their lives. She could feel the tears welling up. Den touched her arm and she looked up at her lover, glad that she was there. And now, when she thought she would break down completely, Den surprised her further by saying to her dad, "So, Mr Moss, who's going to win the Open this year? Any bets on Rory McIlroy?"

She sat back and watched in wonder and relief as Den engaged her father in a spirited discussion on the forthcoming golf tournament.

†

Soames settled down on a favoured perch by the door with the sunlight streaming in. The large ginger cat often accompanied her when she was painting. His mother, Fleur, was the more energetic of the two during the day and was likely prowling the field looking for mice.

The three days away from the farm had seemed like two weeks, almost like a holiday. For now Ellie was pleased to be back, getting into her regular routine. An idea for a new painting was drifting about in her subconscious waiting for her to pick up a brush.

What had sparked the image in her mind? Recalling their early morning lovemaking, she experienced a rush of heat between her legs and down her thighs with the memory of Robin's tongue stroking her towards another climax. Robin's arms held her close afterwards as her heartbeat returned to normal.

Weren't women over fifty supposed to be past any kind of lust-filled sessions? From what she read in newspapers and magazines, she wasn't normal. But who was to say what was normal. According to received wisdom, she was now in the crone stage of the female life cycle. Menopause had passed her by. One day her periods just stopped. There was no transition phase, no hot flushes or weird food cravings. She had decided the best approach to this phase of life was to embrace the inner crone. Perhaps she should give seminars. Who said crones couldn't have fun? Who said crones couldn't be sexy?

Blue sky, a few fluffy clouds floating by, colours were coming through her thoughts, wanting to be released onto the blank canvas. The vague image that had been at the back of her mind started to take shape.

Before she could make a single brush stroke, the morning peace was shattered by a ringing noise. Soames jumped up and looked at her accusingly. She scrambled for the phone lying on the table. Since the events of the year before when she had found herself cut off from the rest of the world, Robin had insisted she keep the mobile with her, charged up, at all times. When she was at work in the studio she would have preferred to leave it in a drawer in the kitchen.

Looking at the display she saw it was Den calling. She put it to her ear and it kept ringing. *Oh, damn.* She remembered now that she had to swipe something on the device.

"Hello."

"Ellie?"

"Yes."

"Sorry to bother you. I'm on my way over from Blackpool. Long story. Should be with you in about an hour. Is that okay?"

"Yes, that's fine. Are you all right?"

"Yeah, I'm good. Look, I'll see you soon. Bye."

Ellie looked at the screen as the call ended. Did she have to swipe or push anything else? No, it had gone off.

Nine o'clock. Robin had gone for a long bike ride and probably wouldn't be back before lunch. Wondering what Den wanted, Ellie decided to try to capture the image again in the hour of peace she had left.

✝

Jasmine took up Steph's offer to drive her to her flat to pick up more clothes, makeup and post. The gardener sat on her bed watching her select the required cosmetics from her dressing table.

"You really don't need that stuff, Jas."

"Yes, I do. I'll be forty-six on my next birthday." Jas rummaged through her drawer looking for the new eyeliner she'd bought a few weeks ago.

"Well, in my opinion, you really don't."

She had finished loading up the suitcase with her clothes when she spotted the bag in the bottom of the closet. She picked it up and deposited it in the case.

"What's that?" asked Steph.

"Oh, just something I got for a friend."

"So, why are you looking shifty?" Steph reached into the bag and pulled out the box. "Hm. This looks interesting. I know that logo."

Jas grabbed at the box to pull it out of Steph's hands and the dildo flew out landing on the floor between them.

"Ooh, you are quite the dark horse, Jas. I bet you didn't really need anything else here. You just came back for this." Steph picked it up before Jas could react. "Who's the lucky friend?"

Jas couldn't stop the blush that was creeping up her neck into her face. Ever since the night before when first Steph had massaged her shoulders and she had returned the favour, images of Steph's strong hands massaging other parts of her body beset her.

"It looks like it hasn't been used. Probably needs a test run, don't you think? You'd want to check it works properly before giving it to your friend?" Steph placed a heavy emphasis on the word 'friend' and winked at her.

"Steph!" Jas grabbed the dildo back and placed it in the suitcase. "I've finished in here. I'll just look at the post and check my messages, then we can go."

The post contained an invitation in a gold embossed envelope and Jasmine had a good idea what it was before pulling the card out. She stared at the invitation in dismay. Her young cousin, Emma, was getting married and had finally got around to sending out invites. When she checked her messages, there was only the one from her mother saying how much they were looking forward to the wedding and they hoped she would bring her new beau, Max. And would they get to meet him before the wedding? The invitation coupled with the phone message from her mother was enough to make anyone despair.

Steph had heard the last part of the message as she carried the suitcase into the hallway.

"Seems like now might be a good time to let them in on your deep dark secret."

"I don't know, Steph. Whenever I'm there, I just can't seem to find the right time to do it."

"And now they think you're involved with a man. With Max, even. Look, what's the worst that can happen? They'll never speak to you again? You're their only child, right? So, that's not too likely. It might take them a bit of time to come to terms with it, but I don't think they'll cut you off."

"You don't know them."

"For God's sake, Jas. You're forty-five years old. You don't need permission from your parents to do anything."

Jas looked down at the floor, close to tears. She knew Steph was right. It was an unnecessary burden she'd been carrying around. It was time to unload it.

†

It had been a wrench leaving Kathryn's bed that morning. They had talked long into the night and reached an agreement about their respective living arrangements. Den would talk to her editor about working from a northern base and if that didn't seem feasible, she thought she could freelance for a while. Kathryn's lecture time at the university wouldn't start until October and she would need to be in London some of the time during August and September preparing for the exhibition. Den had suggested they co-opt Jas into helping with the organisation as neither of them could be on hand for day-to-day liaison with the museum.

The only sticking point had been when Kathryn mentioned Ellie's painting and how much she wanted it.

"I know you hate the idea of me seeing her again, but I need to ask if she will sell it?"

"She's already told you it's not for sale. I think it would be better if I go and see her. She still might not sell it, but I may be able to negotiate a loan."

They had talked it back and forth and finally Kathryn agreed to let Den go and talk to Ellie. She planned on staying in Lytham until the weekend when her father was due to be released. Once he was settled, she would be going back to Durham. She had shown Den photos of the flat she had put an offer on, enthusing about the views and the proximity to the city centre and the university.

"It looks great, but I thought we were going house hunting together."

"I didn't think you were that interested and when I saw this online, it looked too good to pass up."

"Is it big enough for both of us to live there?" When Kathryn nodded, Den hugged her and said, "Then it's fine with me."

Den hadn't seen much of Kathryn's mother and had the feeling the woman was avoiding her. "I don't think she approves of me," she said to Kathryn as she was getting dressed.

"She'll come round. Losing the match on the eighteenth hole yesterday has upset her more than she'll let on."

"Oh. I thought she might be upset about your dad being in hospital."

"Not really. Now they know what it is and how to treat it." Kathryn still sounded sleepy.

Den bent over the bed and kissed her brow. "Get some more rest, love. I'll ring you after I've talked to Ellie."

Now as she headed up the long track to Starling Hill farm she wondered how best to approach the artist. If Robin were around she might be able to enlist her support. But as she reached the farmyard she saw that the motorcycle was missing from its usual space. Well, she was going to have to go it alone and hope for the best.

Ellie emerged from the studio wiping her hands on her paint-covered T-shirt. It looked like one of Robin's old ones as it came down to her knees. Den got out of the car and stretched her legs. Her neck was stiff and her shoulders felt like they did after hours of typing. It wasn't the driving, she thought, so much as the apprehension of how Ellie might re-act when she knew the reason for her visit. And she didn't want to have to face a disappointed Kathryn when Ellie said no.

Taking a deep breath of the fresh country air, Den smiled at Ellie and headed across the yard towards her.

"Sorry to interrupt your day. Were you in the middle of something?" Bit of a stupid question she realised, as soon as the words left her mouth. Of course Ellie was in the middle of something. She'd been painting and Den knew only too well what it was like to be distracted when trying to finish an article.

Ellie shook her head. "It's okay. I could do with a break now anyway. Come on in and I'll put the coffee on."

✝

"Nice wheels," Ellie said as she moved around the big farm kitchen. "I didn't get a proper look at your car before."

"It's not mine. If I had a car, it wouldn't be one of those. It's nice to drive but a monstrous gas guzzler."

"So, what's the long story?"

Den looked at her, puzzled.

"How did you end up in Blackpool?"

"Oh, right." Den gave her a condensed version of events, leaving out the fact that she and Kathryn had spent the night at the hotel in Durham in separate bedrooms.

"And he's going to be okay, is he?"

"Yes. They've done all the tests and he'll be on warfarin for six months. He's been told to walk every day but that's not a problem as he's a rabid golfer. Well, both her parents are."

"So, are you on your way back to London or Durham?"

"I'm going back to London. Henry's getting anxious about PJ." The ginger cat had followed them into the kitchen and was staring up at her from the floor.

"PJ?"

"The car. His pride and joy." The cat jumped up onto her lap, demanding to be stroked. He settled down with a soft purr when she obliged.

"Okay. I know this isn't the shortest route to London from Blackpool, so what gives?"

Den looked over at Ellie who was giving her a cat-like stare. *She knows*, she thought. *Might as well get straight to the point.* "It's about the painting, the one Kathryn wanted to buy." Den swallowed. "I know you don't want to sell it. But would you consider loaning it...just for the duration of the

183

exhibition at the British Museum? It would be quite a coup for you, as an artist."

The silence lengthened. Ellie was tracing a pattern on the tabletop. Den scratched behind the cat's ears and his purring was the loudest noise in the room. Her legs were starting to cramp before Ellie spoke. She gently placed the cat on the floor. He looked up at her accusingly and stalked off.

"How would it be used?" Ellie asked finally.

"I'm not really sure. I don't know how these things work. They'll be exhibiting the two main skeletons, and I guess the picture would be part of the display, maybe. An artist's impression of what they looked like."

"I've been told they've done facial reconstructions from the skulls."

"Who told you that?"

"Ed McLaughlin keeps me informed. As the osteo-archaeologist on the dig, he has been involved with making sure the bones were aligned properly for the displays. So I don't see why they would need my picture. They'll have 3D representations of the heads, more lifelike and probably much more accurate than my interpretation."

"It's such a strong image, Ellie. I can see why Kathryn's taken with it. It may be they will want to use it for publicity purposes. You know, those big banners that hang outside the entrances to the exhibit halls, posters at tube stations, that sort of thing." Den wondered if she'd gone too far. Ellie wasn't likely to be swayed by the thought of becoming a household name. She had welcomed a return to her quiet life when the dig shut down but the exhibition would bring it all to the fore again with more unwanted media attention. Den had almost given up hope of any answer before Ellie spoke again.

"They would have to pay me for that kind of usage."

"Can I take that as a yes?"

"I know I'm probably going to regret this, but yes on one condition."

"Anything you say." Relief coursed through Den's body.

"The agreement will be with the museum's curators through Ed. I don't want any personal contact with Kathryn."

Den sighed. This was fine with her but she wasn't sure how Kathryn would take it. She understood the message only too well and was now glad that Robin hadn't been present for this discussion. She took another deep breath. "Okay. Well, that's great."

"I'll talk to Ed. You can let Kathryn know it's happening."

"Thanks. She will be extremely grateful."

"And, as far as Robin's concerned, we haven't had this conversation."

Den wasn't happy about deceiving the woman she had come to regard as a good friend, but she agreed. If this was part of the deal, then it had to be done. Her main concern was giving Kathryn what she wanted and she was relieved to be driving away from the farm with mission accomplished. Thankful once again for the gadgetry in Henry's pride and joy, she plugged her phone into the Bluetooth and rang Kathryn as she negotiated the narrow roads leading back to the motorway.

Kathryn picked up right away.

"Okay. It's a deal."

"Fantastic. Well done."

"She is happy to loan it to the museum and said she'll ask Ed to liaise with the curators." Den hoped this didn't sound too much like a snub.

"Oh."

That one syllable told Den that Kathryn wasn't fooled. She tried to soften the blow with her next words.

"Look, love, you know how publicity-shy she is. If that's how she wants to do it, I don't think we should push it. The fact that she's agreed at all is amazing."

"Right. Okay, well, thanks for doing that."

"It wasn't the easiest of conversations. You owe me one."

"One what?"

"I'll let you know next time I see you. Gotta go, coming up to the motorway. Love you."

"Love you too. Drive carefully."

Den smiled as she turned up the car's sound system. Somehow the journey south didn't seem so lonely this time.

†

When she had lugged the suitcase up the stairs, Steph sat on the bed and watched Jasmine unload her stuff. It wasn't right to take advantage of a woman in a weakened state of mind, but she thought Jas was probably over the worst of it. She knew if she didn't make a move soon she would lose her nerve.

"Thirsty work, moving," she said finally. "Want a beer?"

"Sure. But I don't think I can make it down those stairs again right now."

"That's okay." Steph bounced up off the bed. "I'll be right back."

On the way back up with the bottles, she stopped by her room. Reaching into the back of her sock drawer she found what she was looking for. The leather was supple and pliant. She hadn't worn the harness for some time but it felt smooth against her skin as she buckled it on and pulled her shorts back up. Now or never, she said to herself as she walked slowly up the stairs to Den's room, her hot hands making the cold beer bottles sweat.

Jasmine was lying back on the bed, one arm over her eyes. Her breasts were moving up and down with her shallow breaths. Steph put the bottles down by the bed and went over to the suitcase. Jasmine had left it open and the dildo was nestled in a pile of knickers. With a practiced move, Steph inserted it into the hole in the harness and adjusted her shorts. This was going to be fun, she hoped.

"What are you doing?" Jasmine was sitting up, watching her over the rim of her beer bottle.

"Just preparing a little treat for you." Steph walked over to the bed awkwardly. She leaned over and kissed Jasmine on the lips. She met with no resistance and after a brief pause, Jas responded, opening her mouth slightly to let Steph explore with her tongue. As they moved onto the bed, with Steph on top, Jasmine let out a gasp. She had felt the length of the object against her leg.

Steph grinned down at her. "Just testing it out for your friend."

"You're so thoughtful." Jasmine gave her the kind of lust-filled look she had been hoping for and grasped her shoulders to pull her closer.

†

The long drive had been made longer with the accident on the motorway just past Nottingham. The collision had been on the northbound carriageway but the rubberneckers slowed it down for the London-bound stream as well.

Den was looking forward to falling into her own bed after six hours on the road. She could hear voices in the kitchen but she really didn't want to have to speak to anyone. Dropping the car keys in their dish by the front door she crept up the stairs feeling older with each step. The idea of living in a flat, even if it was in Durham, held a lot of appeal she thought as she approached the top floor and her own welcoming space.

Reaching the top at last, she pushed open the door to her room and stopped. There were two bodies on the bed; both butt naked and engaged in an intense form of sexual activity. She closed the door quietly and made her way wearily back down the stairs.

Henry and Paul were in the kitchen in their familiar places. Henry was doing something unspeakable to a chicken and Paul was sitting on a stool by the counter watching his lover and sipping on a cup of tea.

"Hey, Den. Didn't hear you come in. Everything okay?" Henry greeted her, looking up from his eviscerations.

"Yeah. Just dandy. I've driven the length and breadth of the country in the last few days and I get home to find two women fucking in my bed."

"Oh my God!" Paul raised his arms in mock horror. "Call pest control. An infestation of lesbians! I warned you, Hen. You let one in and before you know it, they're everywhere…"

"Shut up, Paul. Who the fuck are they? And why are they in my room?"

"You better sit down and have a drink. It's a long story. Paul, is there any of that Glenfiddich left. I think Den needs a booster."

Paul fetched a large glass of whisky and sat back down as Henry brought her up to date with local events.

"Jas and Steph! You've got to be kidding!"

"No, not kidding. I could see Steph was getting a bit love-struck. But I didn't think anything would come of it." Henry finished stuffing the chicken and went over to the sink to wash his hands.

"Last time I saw Jas, she was over the moon with this new woman in her life, someone she met through work I thought."

"Well, I guess it all went tits up, so to speak. She hasn't said much about it to either of us. I would guess Steph knows more."

"They weren't exactly talking upstairs! Their mouths were otherwise engaged."

"Eww! Too much information." Paul pinched her arm.

"Anyway, come on Den. We want to hear all about your adventures up north." Henry smiled at her.

"Another time, guys. I'm whacked out. Where am I supposed to sleep?"

"Well, I guess Steph's bed is free."

"Get real, Hen. It's probably full of maggots or weeds."

"All right, Miss Fussy. Come on Paul. We'll do our housemaid act and change the sheets."

Den was too tired to argue. She let them make up the bed for her, then fell into it. But before she could fall asleep she wanted to talk to Kathryn.

✝

When the phone rang Kathryn was just thinking of turning in, having exhausted what little conversation she could manage with her mother. There was only so much time she wanted to spend listening to her describe her golf round hole by hole.

"It's Den," she said and moved into the kitchen to talk.

She listened to Den's tales of woe. "But Henry's looking after you, I guess."

"Yeah, of course. How's Howie?"

Kathryn laughed. No one had ever called her father that, but when Den did he didn't seem to mind. Just as she didn't when Den called her Kat. "Still thinks he'll be out splitting the fairways with his driver on the weekend."

"I love it when you talk dirty."

"When did you become such an expert on golf?"

"I read a lot."

"He thinks you're wonderful.

"Good. He doesn't mind us shacking up together, then?"

"No. I didn't think he would. Anyway, listen. I've got some good news." Kathryn had received a call from the university's admin office that afternoon. They were able to offer her temporary accommodation in University College quarters located in the castle. She would be able to stay there until the new term started. "Hopefully I'll have completed on the flat by that time."

They talked for a bit longer until Kathryn sensed that Den was fading on the other end. Finishing the call she felt as if a weight had lifted off her shoulders. It was, she realised, nice to have the connection with someone who cared, someone who wanted to share the minutiae of her daily life. Maybe she could get the hang of this relationship business after all.

Chapter Nine

Deadlines

What a difference a month could make. Jas couldn't believe the number of life changes she had made in a few short weeks. First and foremost, she was setting up home with Steph. This had required negotiating with Den about swapping rooms. She hadn't been looking forward to that conversation, knowing how much Den loved her space at the top of the house. But Den had surprised her by saying it wasn't a problem. She was going to be spending most of her time in Durham with Kathryn and only wanted to keep a room in the house for the occasional visits to London.

It was a marvellous feeling, being in love and feeling so totally loved in return. She had never experienced anything like it. She knew she had found a soul mate in Steph. There was so much still to explore in their relationship but she knew she could trust her. Steph had taken her time, testing what she wanted, what she could give her, what she could take. She knew she was safe.

Her first day back at work after her week off had been uncomfortable. Her boss called her into his office before she'd had time to switch on her computer. He wanted to know why they had suddenly lost the Fleetwood account. And was it anything to do with her going AWOL the past week?

191

"I was ill," she had countered.

"You look well enough to me. In fact, you look like you've been on holiday."

Jas had looked down at herself and thought it was probably true that she was looking healthier than she had for some time. She had spent long hours outside during the week, either helping Steph with gardening projects or taking walks by the river and sitting in the park. It had been like a holiday. And the memory of the night before in bed with the energetic gardener brought a smile to her face.

"What are you grinning about?" he had barked at her. "This is no laughing matter. That account was worth a lot to Armadillo."

Two days later, having talked it over with Steph, she handed in her notice. Her assistant, Ray, had been taken aback by the sudden announcement of her intention to quit but she told him she had been unhappy with the job for a while. Now was a good opportunity to take some time out and think about setting up her own business.

Another major decision had been to sell her flat and this was something else she would have to tell her parents when the time came.

✝

Den stood by the window watching the rain. It had all happened so quickly but she couldn't help smiling at her own acceptance of the changes. She had never thought she would ever want to leave London and yet here she was looking forward to it. The large rucksack by the door held everything she needed for the next few weeks. Henry and Paul would bring the remaining books and winter clothes when they came for their first visit. Her life in so few containers...one backpack, three boxes of books and a suitcase. How did she manage to reach the age of forty-five with so few material possessions to show for it? No car, no mortgage, no furniture even.

She was waiting for Henry to accompany her to the train station. His plans for the day included meeting friends for lunch uptown but he wanted to see her off first.

"Taxi's here," he called from the hallway.

She joined him and picked up her rucksack, silently saying goodbye to the house that had been home for so many years.

They settled into their seats and Henry took her hand.

"I'm going to miss you."

"It's not the other side of the world. And you're coming to visit soon."

"You really think the professor's ready for this. Does she know what she's letting herself in for?"

"Maybe not, but she's stuck with me."

They both looked out of the window at the passing traffic. Den knew that once she was on the train heading north she would be fine. It was really happening. She was moving in with Kathryn.

"I want to marry her, Henry."

"Jesus, Den. Don't you think you should wait a bit? See how living together pans out. From what you've said, Kathryn gets spooked by the love word, never mind anything like lifelong commitment."

"It just feels so right."

"To you, maybe. I think you should take it slowly. Give her time."

The traffic was crawling slowly towards the West End now. The driver took the road through the park to try and dodge some of the heavier congestion. But she wasn't worried about missing the train, they had left plenty of time for the journey to King's Cross.

†

Moving day. Kathryn couldn't believe it was happening. The sale had gone through a lot faster than she could have expected. After collecting the keys from the estate agent, she had driven over to the flat and sat in her car wondering if she had done the right thing. The removal van would be arriving soon and Den was on the train.

The last few weeks had shot by. She had immersed herself in the dig at Binchester and joined the team in cataloguing and analysing the finds. Having accommodation in the castle, even though it was a cramped student room, had been wonderful. She had been able to explore the city and familiarise herself with the layout of the main university campus. Spending time with her new colleagues had also been useful. She felt they were still tiptoeing around one another, but once the term started she was sure she would start to feel part of the team.

Going back to Huddersfield to say goodbye to Ed and other staff she had worked with closely for the past eight years, nostalgia overcame her. Saying a final goodbye to the house, once the last of the boxes had been loaded onto the van, had been a more emotional experience than she expected.

More than a few times during those final days in her old home, she had considered making one last trip to Starling Hill. She had even got halfway there one evening before turning around and heading back. Den had called that night, as if sensing from two hundred miles away that her thoughts were wandering. She appreciated Den's support, even from a distance, and she was looking forward to seeing her again. But she had the guilty feeling she hadn't been as supportive to her as she should have been.

Wrapped up in her own worries she hadn't given any thought to what Den was dealing with. The reporter didn't say much, just that she had exchanged rooms with Steph so that the new couple could have more space. She also related that her editor had told her to "fuck off" when she told him she was moving north. But then he called the next day to say he would expect her to send any articles to him first. Den seemed happy to be going freelance, but Kathryn suspected it wasn't going to be easy for her.

If moving out of the house had been traumatic, she wasn't prepared for the emotion of finding herself in the new flat, surrounded by boxes and furniture in odd places. The thought of unpacking was depressing. Having the weekend to get sorted out had seemed doable when planning the move but now she was wondering if it had all been one big mistake.

†

Steph was glad her prediction had come true. Jasmine had been fretting all week about what the weather would be like for the wedding and the day had turned out fine, which is what she had told her days ago. *Trust me, I'm a gardener*, she had joked with her. But Steph knew the weather question was only a cover for the real anxiety—finally coming out to her parents. Not only that but introducing them to her lover.

It was a big day in the life of her cousin, but an even bigger day for Jas. Steph checked her outfit. She hadn't wanted to upstage the groom by wearing a full tux so she had opted for a jazzy waistcoat and western-style string tie to go with her black pleated trousers and purple shirt. The only problem was she now looked like a blackjack dealer in a casino. Anyway, Jas's approval was all that mattered and she liked the look. Henry had been persuaded to lend her his car.

It would help, she explained, to give a good impression, rather than arriving in her beat-up work van.

Jasmine emerged from the bathroom with five minutes to spare before they needed to set off. She looked stunning in a summer print sheath dress Steph hadn't seen before. With her release from the office routine and the exercise she was getting on a nightly basis, she had shed a good stone and a half and was looking great.

She shimmied over to Steph and put her hand on her belt. "Do you like what you see, hon?"

Steph swallowed and nodded. Jas took one of Steph's hands and moved it onto her butt. Steph could feel the rounded mound through the silkiness of the material moving gently under her fingers. "Are you still sore, babe?"

"Not sore enough. I'll be in need of a good spanking after this." Jas's lips quivered over her ear.

"Jas! If you don't stop teasing me, we won't make it to this wedding."

Her lover laughed and slid out of her grasp. "You look so hot in that outfit, I couldn't resist."

Steph was tempted to say, *fuck the wedding, let's go to bed.* Instead she took Jas's hand in hers and said, "Come on, then. When this shindig's over, you will get what's coming to you, I promise."

"I'll hold you to that, sweetheart."

They pulled up to the country house hotel with only a few minutes to go before the start of the ceremony. Steph was able to find a space on the grass not far from the entrance, ever mindful of Henry's instructions about taking care of the paintwork. She opened the passenger door for Jas and helped her steady herself. The high heels she was wearing looked impossible to walk in but she managed it with an ease that Steph could only marvel at.

They were directed to seats only a few rows back from the front of the room. Jas pointed out the backs of her parents' heads as they sat down.

†

Den looked down at the city from the train station. She had left the rain behind in London. It was a bright, breezy day up here in the northeast. The top of the castle was visible above the trees on the other side of the steep gorge, and further along the more imposing structure of the cathedral.

She started down the steps. It seemed a long way down to the main road leading into the city. She followed it round to the bridge and was immediately transported into another country. Large flower displays adorned the bridge, an accordion player was playing recognisable tunes and some people stopped to listen and drop coins into his hat. *Another accordion player, another time.* Den smiled at the memory and found loose change in the pocket of her jeans.

The road on the other side of the bridge led up to the market square where there was a group busking and crowds enjoying the music and the sunshine. The place was busy now with tourists—she couldn't imagine being able to move in the narrow streets once the university students arrived for the start of term.

The apartment building looked very new but built from the same type of sandstone as the castle and blended in with the older dwellings on the street. She pushed the buzzer for Flat 1 and the answering buzz let her push the door open.

When she arrived in the living room, Kathryn was standing by the window gazing down at the river.

"You got my text, then. I'm guessing you don't just open the door for anyone." Den dumped her heavy rucksack on the floor. The room was filled with boxes.

Kathryn turned towards her and Den could see she was struggling with something. Take it slowly, Henry had said. Den took a deep breath and went over to the window. She stood next to the professor and looked out. It was a great view, the main selling point for the flat.

"Kat, talk to me." Den was learning the best way to handle the professor at times like this. She was grateful for Howard Moss's helpful advice to try and get his daughter to speak when she went quiet.

"It's such a mess. I don't know where to start."

"Good thing I'm here, isn't it? Show me where you want your computer set up and put this in the fridge." She opened the top of her rucksack and pulled out the bottle of Veuve Clicquot purchased on her way through the square. "I'm hoping the fridge is here and plugged in."

Kathryn cracked a brief smile and nodded.

They worked together for an hour. It took Den a while to get the Wi-Fi router set up and configure the computer settings. Kathryn was sorting through books and putting them on shelves. When Den checked on her she was staring into one of the boxes and had only lined up half a dozen books on one shelf. Others were piled up randomly.

"I knew I should have packed these myself."

"What's the matter? They're not damaged, are they?"

"No. But they're all mixed up. It's going to take ages to put them in order."

Den wasn't so fussy about her own bookshelves but she could usually put her hand on any book she wanted. Kathryn, she suspected, would have all her books in a methodical order, alphabetical or some academically archaic system that would only make sense to her.

"How about we take a break? The books will still be here and I think we could both do with a glass of champagne."

"Um…" Kathryn looked around helplessly.

"The glasses are still in a box? Not to worry. I've always wanted to swig Champers out of the bottle, like I've just won Wimbledon or something."

After a few slugs of the bubbly drink, Den led the professor into the only room with a bed in it and started to undress her. Kathryn put a hand on her chest.

"We don't have time for this."

"We have all the time in the world, my love." Den embraced her and kissed her already yielding lips. The lack of resistance encouraged her to move one of her hands down to Kathryn's bottom and trap one of her legs between hers. It reminded her of the first time they'd had sex, shortly after they had met, when she pushed Kathryn up against the hotel door. The professor was responding now as she had then, her hands finding their way under her shirt, her heart pounding, breathing rapidly. This wasn't turning out to be the leisurely lovemaking session Den had visualised in her head during the long train journey. But it was a good start.

✝

The pile of books didn't look any smaller. After making love the previous afternoon, Den had told her to leave the books so they could sort out the kitchen. While she didn't mind drinking out of a bottle, she thought it might be useful to find the plates and the cutlery. They had eaten Indian takeaway sitting on the floor of the living room, watching the fading light on the river. And after that, Den had taken her back to bed again.

This morning Kathryn had woken to find the bed empty. She had a dim memory of her lover saying something about getting a Sunday paper. After a quick shower, dressed in a loose T-shirt and shorts, she walked into the room designated as her office and surveyed the open boxes and the random piles of books littering the floor with dismay. Den appeared in the doorway with an armful of newspapers.

"Ready for breakfast?"

Kathryn waved at the disorganised clutter surrounding her. "I need to do something with these."

"Coffee, food, read the paper…in that order. Then I'll help you with the books."

"Where did this bossy streak come from?"

"Must have caught it from you, Professor." Den grinned at her; the captivating grin that had inflamed her interest in the journalist from the start.

She let Den take charge of their morning. After breakfast, Den helped by putting the books on the shelves once Kathryn had put them in the right order. With her office sorted out, she felt more relaxed and agreed to go out for a walk. The market square was buzzing as usual. She took Den's hand and felt her insides melting when the taller woman looked down at her and smiled. Something was shifting inside her. *Could it be love? Surely not.* That just didn't happen to women at her advanced age, did it?

Without speaking, they walked hand in hand through the square and down the cobbled street to the narrow steps leading down to the river. When they were out of sight of the bridge and next to some overhanging trees, Den stopped and pulled her into an embrace. Kathryn found herself responding. She wasn't used to this. She just felt incredibly sexy and wanted Den to make love to her right there on the path. *This is what horny teenagers do, not middle-aged professors.* But that thought didn't stop her from pushing her tongue into Den's mouth while grinding her hips against her lover's firmly braced thighs.

A family passed them and the sound of the children giggling brought Kathryn to her senses. "We can't do this here. Take me home."

Den's smile widened. "I like the sound of that."

†

The wedding ceremony itself passed in a blur. Jasmine grasped Steph's hand as soon as they sat down and didn't let go throughout the young couple's exchange of vows. If Steph felt any discomfort, she didn't show it and Jas marvelled again at how lucky she was to have her in her life. The interlude, one-sided games of power with Max Fleetwood, would most likely have ended in disaster anyway. But she didn't regret it. How could she? Those few sessions with Max had released something in her. Desires she knew she had but would never have acted on.

As the newly wed couple walked down the aisle and the first rows stood up to follow, Steph whispered in her ear. "It will be okay. Whatever happens, I'm here."

Jas looked down and unclasping her hand saw the red marks of her nails imprinted in Steph's flesh. "Sorry, babe."

"Don't be. You're mine and that's all that matters."

If they hadn't been forced to get up and follow the flow of guests surging up the aisle, Jas would have kissed her lover then and there. Kissed her so thoroughly they would have been making out in their seats oblivious to the crowd.

Outside the church, Jasmine took a deep breath and looked around for her parents. They were talking to an aunt she vaguely remembered from other family gatherings. Her mother saw her first, smiled and waved her over.

"You look lovely, darling," she said as Jasmine reached her. The aunt moved off to talk to someone else. Her father just nodded. He looked uncomfortable in the morning suit that was probably too tight. Her mother was wearing an outfit that would have been suitable for the mother of the bride but which Jas thought was over the top for one of the bride's aunts. And the feathery fascinator didn't do her any favours,

201

either. She would mention it later, if her mother were still speaking to her.

"Mum, Dad. You both look very smart." She kissed her mother lightly on the cheek, careful not to ruin her makeup or smudge her own lipstick.

"Thank you, dear. Isn't it a wonderful turnout for Emma and...what's the boy's name?"

"Richard." Jas had paid enough attention to the ceremony to know that, at least.

"Oh yes. Silly me. He seems a nice lad. And his family are the right sort, don't you think?"

"I haven't met them."

"No, of course. I'll introduce you."

"That would be nice, Mum. But I'd like to introduce you to someone first." She found Steph's hand and pulled her close. "This is Stephanie Williams."

"Oh, I thought you were bringing someone called Max. We were looking forward to meeting him."

Jas felt Steph stiffen and squeezed her hand. "That didn't work out. Anyway, Steph's my partner. We're living together now."

Steph stepped forward. "Pleased to meet you, Mr and Mrs Pepper."

Jas's mother took a step back. "But you're, you're a woman."

"Yep. Last time I looked, anyway."

Her dad seemed to have found something interesting to look at in the brickwork by the church door while her mother lowered her voice and hissed at her. "Jasmine! How dare you! What were you thinking bringing this...this creature to your cousin's wedding? And what do you mean you're living together? That's absurd. You have a perfectly good flat of your own." Her fascinator wobbled dangerously in a sudden gust of wind.

"I'm selling it, Mum. Oh, and I've left my job as well. I'm going to set up my own business."

"You what? Oh my God! Jeremy, talk some sense into your daughter. She's gone mad. Completely mad." Tears were gathering in her eyes.

"She's old enough to know what she's doing, Joan." He looked at Jasmine and then held his hand out to Steph. "Good luck with this one, Miss Williams. She's a bit of a handful."

"Dad!"

"We better get going. See you at the reception." He took his wife by the arm and led her away.

By the end of the evening, Jasmine was feeling worn out. Steph had spent some time talking to her father and seemed to have won him over. Her mother ignored her completely, making a point of speaking to anyone else in her vicinity.

†

"Your dad's really nice." Steph was concentrating on driving. "He says your mum will come round. She'll just need a bit of time to get used to the idea."

"I'm just glad it's over. I guess it could have been worse." Jas put her hand on Steph's leg, needing to feel the connection with her.

"Sure. Anyway he's invited us to spend Christmas with them."

"Jesus! You two must have really hit it off. You're not taking up golf, are you?"

"No. But he does want some advice on their garden."

Jas watched the road ahead, cars passing them. "He was pretty good about everything. He even said he would send me a list of his contacts if I needed help or ideas for setting up my business."

She slept the rest of the way home, only waking up as Steph stopped the car to park on the street. She leant on her, still sleepy, as they walked up the path to the front door. Once inside, Steph turned off the light, and pushed Jas up against the wall. "I believe I promised you something earlier. And from what your father's told me, you require a lot of discipline."

Jasmine squirmed as Steph pressed her body against hers. She was, suddenly, wide awake again, alive to a flash of desire. "Oh yes, I do. I really do."

Steph released her and gestured for her to go up the stairs in front of her. Jasmine ascended slowly, moving her hips provocatively with each step. She knew by now what drove Steph wild. And she wanted her wild tonight.

†

Ellie offered her visitor a cup of tea and he accepted. They were in the farmhouse kitchen with the chill of a late summer evening offset by the warmth coming from the Aga. The kettle had just been coming to a boil when he arrived.

"We'll take good care of it," he said when she sat down with her own cup.

The painting was safely in the back of Ed McLaughlin's car wrapped and ready for delivery to the museum.

"I know you will. But it will be strange to see it in a different setting."

"You're definitely coming to the opening of the exhibition, then?"

"Yes, of course. Just don't make me talk to any of the press."

"Right. I'll try to keep the vultures at bay." He sipped at his tea. "You know Kathryn's moved now. Her house sold very quickly."

"Yes, I know. Robin and Den keep in touch on Face-book."

They talked for a bit longer about other things, the weather, and the conflicts around the world, the Scottish referendum. After Ed left, Ellie went over to the studio and stood looking at the space where the painting had rested. She was going to miss the queen and her consort. Maybe it was an early sign of dementia; she had often found herself talking to the painting. She did worry that she would inherit her mother's increasing forgetfulness and disappear into the fog of another world. But if that happened she wouldn't know if she couldn't remember. It would be Robin who would. Then again, it was no use worrying about something that might not happen. Robin was there to keep her in the present.

As if on cue, the sound of the motorbike on the track reached her ears. She smiled, looked at the empty space, and just nodded to it. The queen had found her peace here with her lover, and so had she.

Jen Silver

Epilogue

Any Other Business

Kathryn stayed back in the shadows watching people as they moved through the exhibition. The skeletons drew a lot of attention, of course, but the case displaying the 3D representations of the heads of Queen Cartimandua and Vellocatus held an almost hypnotic fascination for the viewers. She wouldn't have described the queen as beautiful from the reconstructed image, but there was a sense of a woman used to wielding power. On the advice of one of the museum's Roman experts, Vellocatus had been given the short military hairstyle of a legionnaire and it wasn't hard to see how she could have passed as a man. The bones in the case were indicative of a tall person and there were marks on her arms and legs that showed someone who was battle-scarred.

There were times in the past few weeks when she had wondered whether anyone would want to come and view a few old bones and first century artefacts. But the museum's publicity machine had gone to work and the exhibition was fully booked up to Christmas. They were even talking about extending the display for another four months. None of the information given out so far had mentioned the lesbian connection, nor had the news leaked out during the preparations. But they were expecting a media frenzy after this evening's opening event. Jasmine had crafted press releases that she would be activating as soon as the first mention appeared on social media sites. Den had also written an in-depth article, which would appear as a feature in a Sunday newspaper. The more sensational headlines were likely to be along the lines of…"Queen comes out of the closet" and in smaller print "2000 years later." Jas had joked about the lengths some people would go to avoid having to tell their parents.

She had been looking forward to this evening but now she just wanted to get it over with. There were people she would have to speak to, many of them other archaeologists. Her calendar had filled up for the next year with speaking engagements and two overseas conferences. One in Stockholm, which wasn't too bad, but the other was in Sydney—a trip to the other side of the world. Den had said she would come with her and they could turn it into a holiday.

She recalled the meeting with Den's parents earlier in the day. They had made the journey by train from Poole to spend a few days in London and take in the exhibition later in the week. She'd had a lengthy conversation with Den's father, a retired systems analyst. He greeted her as if she were a long-lost relative, welcoming her to the family. And he had warned her about Den saying, "She was an awkward child, stubborn as hell. Tell her not to do something and she would go out of her way to do it. But she is intensely loyal to her friends and family."

Luckily Den had been out of earshot when he told her this. Then her mother had buttonholed Kathryn later to let her know she was glad Den had found someone to settle down with. The implication was that she had passed the parental inspection by having a good job in a respectable profession. They had, her mother went on, been worried about Den. After all, her sister had been happily married for twenty years now. And while they knew Den wasn't going to produce any grandchildren for them, it was all right. They just wanted her to be happy.

Kathryn glanced around, noting the press of people gathered around the painting on the wall near the 3D display. It would be the enduring image for the exhibition, she knew, whether Ellie liked it or not. The museum's shop had postcards, posters, T-shirts and mugs in stock.

"Kathryn! Why are you hiding away back here?"

She smiled at Henry's enthusiastic greeting. "I feel like I've done my bit. This is Cazza and Vee's coming out party. Anyway, glad you could make it. Is Paul here?"

"No, he had to work. Tried to change shifts, but it didn't pan out. He was mad as hell."

"I know it's booked up, but I can get comps for you."

"Oh, that would be wonderful. He'll be thrilled."

"Didn't Den come with you?" They had split up after dinner at Henry's, as Kathryn wanted to be at the museum early to do final checks on the exhibits.

"Yeah. But she and Jas are huddled over her laptop. They're monitoring Twitter and Facebook feeds. I left Steph by the heads. They're amazing reconstructions, aren't they? I didn't know they could do that."

"Well, they do it like this…" Kathryn started but the arrival of Ed and Kieran stopped her.

†

The huge banner swaying in the breeze outside the building caught Ellie by surprise. She had seen photos on the website, but the size of it in real life took her breath away. Robin paid the taxi driver and took her by the arm.

"Are you ready for this?"

Ellie nodded although her insides were churning. Ed had wanted to prepare her for the impact of seeing the two women come to life. On several recent visits to the farm he had offered to show her photos of the reconstructions but she had told him she would wait and see them in person, so to speak, at the opening.

Robin gave her a hug, sensing her nervousness. "It's okay, love. If it gets to be too much, we can leave."

She nodded again and wondered if she would be able to find her voice at all.

There was a large crowd gathered around the skeleton cases. In a separate room, a video loop was playing and a number of people were sitting on the benches watching the unfolding story of the Starling Hill discoveries. But it wasn't hard to work out that the biggest draw was the 3D reconstructions of the heads. Robin, with her height, was able to see the faces before Ellie.

"Stay close," she whispered. "I'll get us to the front."

Ellie held on to her as Robin pushed her way through, politely asking people to move aside.

Finally face-to-face with the queen and her consort, Ellie gasped. "Yes, oh yes!" She clapped her hands, childlike in her wonder. "That's how I saw them, exactly that."

It took all her self-control not to speak to them, the way she had been talking to her painting for months. She looked into the queen's eyes and felt the connection again. An arc over time, the queen and her lover honoured at last.

†

Henry left Kathryn talking to the two men and wandered around the exhibits again. He would enjoy bringing Paul and showing off what he now knew about this period of time. Although Paul had avidly read everything Den had written about Starling Hill and probably knew as much as he did.

He looked around for his friend and saw her talking to the couple who had just arrived, a good-looking red-haired woman, the same height as Den and a smaller blonde. *Of course, the women from the farm.* Den had shown him photos of their wedding. Seeing Ellie Winters in the flesh he could understand Den's fear that Kathryn would never completely get over her obsession. She had an ethereal beauty that was timeless. If he had ever been attracted to women, she would be his type.

Den flashed him a grin as he joined their little group. It was good to see her happy, and she had scrubbed up well for the occasion. On his advice she was wearing a black trouser suit with a white shirt, open at the collar. No one would have taken her for the scruffy journalist who had stumbled into the limelight last year by getting lost on Saddleworth Moor. Her editor had made the scathing comment at the time that he wanted a story from her, not for her to become the story.

"How about an introduction, Den?"

"Of course. Robin and Ellie, I would like you to meet my dearest friend, Captain Henry Stamer. He looks good in his pilot's uniform but he wouldn't wear it tonight."

Robin held out her hand and he shook it. "The owner of a white BMW as well. You're a brave man, letting this dick-head drive it."

"Robin! Behave." Ellie stroked her partner's arm.

"No worries. I threatened her with a fate worse than death if anything happened to it. I understand you have a very fine motorbike."

"Yes. Gabriella. It was touch and go for a while, whether I would need to part with her."

"Gabriella?"

"Yeah, I share a birthday with a certain Argentinian tennis player. Quite a looker. The name suited the bike."

"And I get teased for giving my car a name!" Henry smiled at her. "Are you staying in London long?"

"Just a few days. We've left Jo in charge of the farm."

Henry noticed Den's shudder.

"Was that wise? She'll be reading the cats' paws and do-ing tarot readings for the chickens."

He laughed, remembering what Den had told him about her experience on Jo's boat.

"Yeah. Well, we didn't have much choice. Kieran would have done it but he'd already made arrangements with Dr Ed to come along this evening. Anyway, Jo's all right. I'm sure the inhabitants will survive."

Henry noticed that Ellie was quietly looking around dur-ing this exchange. Den also seemed to be on alert. He real-ised they were both tracking Kathryn's movements. Den vis-ibly relaxed when she picked out the professor talking to an-other group of visitors on the other side of the gallery.

"So, what do you think of all this?" he asked Ellie, to try and draw her into the conversation.

"It's amazing to see how it has been put together. Of course I've seen photos of the skeletons, but the heads are so lifelike. I feel like I know them."

"I suppose you do in a way. Your painting is a very powerful rendition as well."

"Thank you."

Ellie's eyes appeared to be glowing but she seemed em-barrassed by the compliment. Yes, he could definitely see why Den was concerned. A person could fall in love with this woman only too easily.

†

Den looked around and saw that people were leaving. The evening was coming to a close. She packed up the laptop when Steph came over to reclaim Jas's attention. Seeing her friend in love was a new experience but one she could now empathise with.

She looked around for Kathryn. From the conversations overheard she knew the exhibition was a success and people who mattered in the academic world, and beyond, were acknowledging the professor's hard work as a triumph. Staying in the background, she enjoyed watching the way Kathryn charmed everyone who spoke to her with her gracious manner and warm smile.

She didn't think she would ever tire of seeing that smile and her lover's habit of pushing her glasses up the bridge of her nose when she was concentrating. Seeing her in a shimmery blue dress was an additional turn-on. The professor didn't like dressing up but no one would have suspected in the way she held herself, moving easily around the room.

Kathryn was saying goodbye to Henry, Steph, and Jas, who were among the last to leave. Ellie and Robin had left already saying they were meeting up with Kieran and Ed at their hotel. Knowing that this was her chance, she joined in seeing her friends out and then led Kathryn into the darkened video room. The loop was off and they were alone.

"What is it, Den? We don't want to get locked in here."

"A night in the museum, huh. What would these bones tell us? That could be interesting."

"Den! I'm tired. I just want to leave now."

"Okay. In a few minutes. There's something I want to say." Den took a deep breath. She had rehearsed this many times in her head, but she didn't know how it was going to come out. She swallowed hard. "Kathryn, do you like living with me?"

"Yes." Kathryn's arm slipped under her jacket and she rested her hand on Den's hip. "I would think I've made that clear."

"I just wondered...what would you think about getting married?"

The silence seemed to stretch out forever. Den thought she could hear the bones in the other room moving. She could certainly feel her own heart pounding.

"Are you proposing to me?"

"Yes."

More silence and Den thought she had stopped breathing. "Kat? Talk to me, please."

"I…well…it's a nice idea. Maybe…sometime…"

Den sighed. It wasn't the answer she'd hoped for, but it wasn't a definite no. She swallowed her disappointment, glad that Kathryn couldn't see her face. They had, after all, come a long way since the beginning of their relationship. Talking to her father that afternoon, he had told her that if this was what she truly wanted she would need to be patient for once in her life.

There was no point spoiling what had been a wonderful evening, a high point for Kathryn in her career. Knowing she had been part of that would have to be enough for now. She moved out of Kathryn's reach and simply said, "All right. Let's go home."

✝

Home was a lot further north. For the night after the opening of the exhibition it was a room in the St Pancras Renaissance Hotel. Kathryn knew Den had booked it to give them some privacy after the event rather than spending the night at Henry's house. During the short taxi ride from the museum, Den kept her face turned away seemingly interested in the passing traffic and the busy streets still full of people. Now, in the room that had two double beds and was large enough for a group of four, Kathryn wondered if it wouldn't have been better to go back to the Chiswick house. Although full of people, in the intimacy of Den's bedroom there, the space between them wouldn't have been so great.

Once again, she realised, she had failed to react the way her lover wanted. Den's timing wasn't great. Seeing Ellie, even from a distance, had brought up feelings she thought had gone. And she hadn't been able to speak to her. She suspected Robin was managing their movements around the gallery to keep Ellie away from her. There always seemed to be a barrier between them.

Now in the hotel room it seemed she would have to be the first to speak. Den dumped her jacket on a chair and stalked over to the window. She was looking at her phone muttering something about the Wi-Fi signal. Kathryn couldn't find the right words. Den had put a huge effort into making this evening special and she was ruining it for her.

There was a knock on the door. As she was nearest Kathryn opened it. A smiling waiter was holding a tray with a bottle of champagne in an ice bucket and two glasses. She stood aside to let him in. After he'd gone the silence only seemed to deepen.

Kathryn desperately wanted to shrug off the dress she was wearing and get into the shower. But she knew she had to say something. She walked over to the table and picked the bottle out of the bucket. "Hm. One of my favourites. Shall I open it?"

"Yeah, sure. Why not?"

"It went well, didn't it?" Kathryn struggled with the foil around the top of the bottle. Den came over and took it out of her hands. She quickly disposed of the foil and the metal ring, popped the cork and poured two glasses. Handing one to Kathryn, she took a quick swig from her own.

"Den. Come and sit down." Kathryn patted the side of the bed nearest to them. She sat and sipped at her drink. After a few moments Den sat next to her leaving a space. "I'm sorry. You caught me by surprise. I guess I've never thought about getting married. It's not you. It's just...it's never crossed my mind. I don't think I'm cut out to be anyone's wife."

"I don't want a wife, Kathryn." Den's voice cracked with emotion. "I want a partner. Someone to share my life with. And, for some reason, I thought that could be you."

"Well, it could be. If you're willing to put up with a long engagement..." Kathryn looked over at her, smiling.

Den put her glass down on the table. "Stay there," she said as she went over to where she'd left her jacket. She rummaged about in the pocket and came up with a small box. Dropping down on one knee in front of Kathryn she held the box out to her. "Will you marry me? We can write our own words for the ceremony. It doesn't need to be all that formal. Just a commitment of some kind. I love you, Kathryn. I want to spend the rest of my life with you..."

"Will you stop babbling if I say yes?"

"Yes."

Heart pounding, touched by Den's declaration of love, Kathryn smiled and said, "Yes."

"Do you mean that, Professor?" Den's anxiety was palpable.

"Yes, I do." She opened the box and looked inside. The setting on the narrow silver band held a row of tiny bright blue gemstones. "Oh my! That's beautiful."

"They're sapphires. For your birth sign, Virgo."

"Really. I didn't think you were into all that star sign stuff."

"No. I got some advice from a friend. And the colour matches your eyes."

Kathryn felt tears welling up. Den took the ring out of the box and slipped it onto her finger. It fit perfectly. She bent forward and cupped Den's face with her hands. "You are full of surprises. I think I could get used to this."

Their kiss seemed to last a lifetime. When they came up for air, Den grinned at her. "So could I. Now, can I help you out of this dress?"

✝

Den could just see the outline of Kathryn's face in the early morning light filtering through the gap in the curtains. The way her lover could switch between hot and cold was baffling but she was learning to live with it. The hot times were worth every minute. She smiled at the memory of that day by the river just after they'd moved in together. Careful not to wake Kathryn, she moved closer, spooning into her naked form, enjoying the warmth and the softness, wanting to savour these moments of bliss.

Another layer had been scraped away. She was getting closer to the box buried in the earth. Remembering Henry's words, *give her time*; she thought she could do that.

The Last Word

Footnote From the Past

The mages of this time gave her eyes. She viewed the procession of admirers as they stood in awe in front of her image. She understood them well, these people from another time. Like her subjects of old they just needed a push or two in the right direction.

She enjoyed the talks shared with that sweet girl, the potter and artist, seeing the vision of love shared emerge on the canvas. That image was now adorning the wall of this fine place, this temple of celebration, a fitting and most royal tribute.

They were learning from her. Some things you can't fight. A queen's duty is to her people, to protect and serve. This she did for thirty years. She didn't agree with everything the Romans brought to the country, but trade was good. It was good for her people. No one could deny that. The Brigantes weren't starved or slaughtered out of existence like some of the lesser tribes.

The people in this time thought themselves sophisticated, more advanced in their concept of civilisation than the people of her time. Yet they worried about the strangest things. The love between two women, for example. The best years of her long life were spent with Vee. Worth giving up her reign and living out her last years as a free woman with the woman she loved. Maybe, in time, these people would let go of their fears and learn to express and value their love, wherever they found it.

The bones in the glass cages drew her attention.

The digger. One day she will understand. One day she will be able to give her heart to the one who loves her. She has given us a life beyond our time. And for that we thank her and wish her well.

The tall one, the wielder of words, she will wait. And she will be rewarded.

The names of Queen Cartimandua and her lover Vellocatus live now in the imagination of the British people. And soon, they too would be going home to their final resting place— their names linked forever—carved in stone.

About the Author

Jen Silver

Jen lives near Hebden Bridge in West Yorkshire with her long-term partner who she married in December 2014. She has always enjoyed reading an eclectic range of genres including sci-fi, fantasy, historical fiction and lesbian fiction. As well as reading and writing, other activities include golf, archery, and taking part in archaeological digs. Jen's debut novel, *Starting Over* was published by Affinity in October 2014.

Contact Jen at jenjsilver@yahoo.co.uk, friend her on Facebook, or visit her blog: https://jenjsilver.wordpress.com

Other Books from Affinity eBook Press

A Walk Away—Lacey Schmidt Kat and Rand's daily worlds are 2,100 miles apart, but something about their meeting on the magical shores of the nation's oldest national park east of the Mississippi sparks questions that neither woman can just walk away without answering. Sometimes chance brings you to the right person to help you resolve some of your baggage, and you learn to like yourself a little more. Kat and Rand are smart enough to recognize this chance in each other, but they also find that there is a catch to every opportunity—walking toward something is always walking away from something else.

Presence—Charlene Neal After catching her husband red-handed in bed with his secretary, Kayleigh Gibbs takes her daughter and her Jeep and flees across the country. She opens up her own veterinarian practice, and they move into an old, secluded farmhouse in Hoekwil, South Africa. At her best friend's housewarming party Kayleigh meets the beautiful and enchanting Rebecca Steward. Rebecca is instantly drawn to Kayleigh, but is still recovering from a breakup—her girlfriend left her for a man. She's afraid of a repeat performance with Kayleigh, and won't pursue a romantic relationship with her, preferring instead to develop a platonic friendship. When odd, inexplicable things start happening on the farmhouse, a terrified Kayleigh turns to Rebecca for comfort, only to find herself developing unexplainable feelings for her new friend. Rebecca, despite her best intentions, is falling in love with Kayleigh. But when Rebecca moves in with Kayleigh to help her get to the bottom of the haunting, she finds more than she bargained for. Can Rebecca and Kayleigh overcome ghosts from the past and their own insecurities, or will a presence from the past tear them apart?

Love Forever, Live Forever—Annette Mori No one forgets their first love. For Nicky, that's Sara, who abruptly disappears one day, leaving only a cryptic letter. That day scarred her soul. When the pain starts to diminish, Nicky begins to get her life back on track until it is derailed once again by an unimaginable twist. Changed forever, Nicky becomes a careless, womanizing nomad known as the Little Wild One, until she meets Annie. Thirteen years later, Nicky's finally settled and happy. Fate intervenes and puts her directly back into the path of her first love, Sara, and the corresponding events send her into a tailspin. Now she must decide—who will be the person she ends up living with and loving forever?

Possessing Morgan—Erica Lawson New York City, in the height of summer. Crime seems to have taken a holiday, and Detective Morgan O'Callaghan is bored, bored, bored. Paperwork is mating and multiplying on her desk, and even a jaywalker is starting to look good. Anything to get her out from behind her desk! Enter Andrea Worthington, Charleston socialite and all-around rich girl, right down to the wealthy fiancé. She's also the new Assistant District Attorney assigned to Morgan's precinct. Their first meeting is like two freight trains crashing head on. Then a high profile, career make-or-break murder case throws them together again. The investigation has barely begun when Andrea becomes the target of a nearly fatal hit-and-run. But was it really aimed at her? Can she and Morgan find the common ground they need to solve the case and stop the attacks, or are the gaps just too wide to bridge?

Twenty-three Miles—Renee MacKenzie Talia Lisher has a long family history of lying, about anything and everything. With her father dead, and her mom gone on a quest to start a new life, Talia struggles to keep in touch with her only remaining family, her incarcerated brother. When Talia sets her sights on Officer Shay Eliot, she vows to stop lying. She starts watching Shay, waiting for just the right circumstances and amount of courage to talk to her. Talia might be watching Shay, but someone in a dark van is watching Talia. Is the mystery driver a dangerous part of her family's past, or is it all just a coincidence? Shay Eliot has left the police force because of what she perceives as a hostile work environment. When a brutal double-murder on the 23-mile-long Colonial Parkway puts the FBI's magnifying glass squarely on her, her alibi comes from an unlikely source – a young woman who has been stalking her. Shay wants to keep her distance from Talia, but once she gets to know the younger woman she can't keep feelings from developing. This is a story about community, and how it comes together in dangerous and devastating times. When you don't know who to trust, you better have friends who will rally around you. Will Talia and Shay find the answers they need to the mystery of the murders on the parkway, or will justice be elusive? Will they survive their quest for the truth?

Confined Spaces—Renee MacKenzie   Andie Waters spends her days pulling waste samples for environmental testing and at night, she tends bar at The Cave, a popular hangout for straights in a small Georgia town. Serial monogamy has grown stale for her, so she's content working to pay off her debts and hanging out with her old hound dog. Or so she thinks, until a beautiful lesbian drops by The Cave. Andie suspects her involvement with the woman will be only temporary. Little does she know no part of her life will be left untouched. Kara Travis likewise anticipates nothing more than a brief fling upon meeting Andie, especially given her reputation as both a personal ice princess and a corporate hatchet wielder for Royal Environmental. What luck to find a hot lesbian bartender in nowhere rural Georgia. Andie and Kara spend a passionate weekend together and find that their notions of no strings attached are far from accurate. Their supposed short-term ideal diversion of a commitment-free romp hits a major complication when they come face-to-face with one another at Royal Environmental's offices Monday morning. While carrying out her duties, Kara discovers crimes being committed by and against Royal Environmental employees. Will Kara be forced to shut down the Georgia Division of the company? If she does, Andie will lose her job. Worse yet, Kara may lose Andie before she's really even sure she's got her. Corporate politics, complicated romance, and long distances conspire to keep Andie and Kara all boxed in. Can love triumph despite the Confined Spaces?

Reece's Star—TJ Vertigo   Reece Corbett watches over the dancers in her gentleman's club with the blue, razor sharp eyes of The Animal. Few know that resting comfortably in her office is her newest love, a tiny MinPin named Smudge. What happened to The Animal, known for her rapacious appetite for women and danger? Faith Ashford is what happened to The Animal. Faith and Reece have been together a while now and they have settled into something resembling domestic bliss. This bliss alarms Reece. It's one thing for Faith to see her softer side, that's vulnerability enough, but to let her friends see it…no. Not the best plan. Under Faith's guiding, loving hand, will Reece successfully traverse the rocky road of emotion and embrace the positive changes in her life? Or will she panic and be unable to control that Animal part of herself? Will she take that next step to declare herself fully capable of love and devotion? This third installment in the popular series that began with *Private Dancer* continues the passionate and often hilarious romance of Reece and Faith as they both grow in love and in trust.

Flight—Renee Mackenzie It's 1983 and Kate Hunter is a student at a small, private college in Virginia. When Lana coaxes her onto the back of her beat-up scooter one night, Kate's education starts to encompass more than just her pre-vet studies. Kate has always done as expected of her, so when she starts staying away from home on weekends to spend time with her new lover it's way out of character for her. Lana is secretive, but Kate accepts things as they are and gives Lana her space. When she feels the sting of betrayal, will she be able to continue giving Lana her privacy? Kate's sister April is a high school student playing with fire as she parties with her older boyfriend, Boyd. After finding someone overdosed the morning after a big party, April grows weary of all the drugs and alcohol. Will she be able to convince Boyd that they should slow down? Will she be able to pull it together before it's too late? Kate and April are forced to face up to events from their younger years, their mother's desertion, and their long-deteriorating relationship with one another. Some lives will be lost and others changed forever when the sisters' lives intersect. Will they be consumed by the wreckage, or will they be able to pick themselves up and take flight?

Reflected Passion—Erica Lawson Where passion, reality, and destiny combine.
Dale Wincott is a 27-year-old woman born into Bostonian wealth and groomed to marry into the social hierarchy. Her mother is a hard-hearted society matriarch, but her father feels for his daughter and helps Dale find a life on her own as a furniture restorer. Françoise Marie Aurélie de Villerey is a 28-year-old Countess, born into the French aristocracy and forced to marry a count much older than herself. For ten years, she was his trophy wife, forced to endure his perverted desires, until the day he finally died. He had broken her emotionally and she no longer cared for what life had to offer, slipping from one sexual partner to another as often as she changed her clothes. Until... that one night when Françoise looked up during a sexual encounter and saw Dale watching her from the mirror. A veritable angel, full of innocence and curiosity, who touched her very soul. Through the mirror, Françoise embraces life anew, while for Dale it is a powerful awakening, forcing her to discover not only her sensual nature, but the inner strength she possesses.

The One—JM Dragon Phil (Philomena) Casters loves her work as a pilot, above everything else in her life except Ming, her married lover. Phil needs to enhance her status in the community before asking Ming to leave behind her wealthy husband. Rosa Moran a teacher, raised by missionaries in China after the death of her parents. She loves the country of her birth and the people. Her English grandfather desperately wants her to live with him to atone for the guilt he feels about the death of her parents. He sends her a letter requesting her to come home. When Phil flies to the mission to deliver the letter to Rosa, neither can envisage the chain of events about to take place. It starts as a collaboration to save four children, leading them to the surreal private paradise of Langshow. Could this be the perfect place for the children and Rosa to settle? Phil is not so sure. Chang, an old friend from Rosa's childhood lives in Langshow and makes no bones about the fact that he wants Rosa. All thoughts of Ming disappear as Phil tries to fight her attraction to Rosa. However there is the little matter of an innocent misunderstanding—Rosa thinks Phil is a man. *The One* is a romance with everything, love, intrigue, misunderstandings with a happy conclusion—the only question—who gets the girl?

The Chronicles of Ratha: Book 2 A Lion Among the Lambs—Erica Lawson It has been three years since Jordana Laren's path first crossed the Noorthi's - three years since she's had a drink, had sex and a life of her own. Her only excitement has been spent keeping up with her two year-old daughter, Rice, who is definitely a chip off the old block. All has been peaceful until one of the colonists becomes sick. Bad news shifts to worse news when the disease spreads through their community. Unable to get proper medicine, Jordana is forced to rely on the Noorthi healers to come up with a cure. Soon the herbs run out, leaving her with no choice but to search for more on the Noorthi home planet. What is supposed to be a simple pick-up flight turns into a nightmare. Can Jordana believe in herself like her Noorthi sisters do? Only then can she fulfill her destiny as The Chosen One. Follow the colorful cast of characters in this action-packed adventure sequel as they traverse the galaxy. Of course, nothing ever goes smoothly when Jordana is involved.

Cowgirl Up—Ali Spooner When the new ranch hand, Coal Bryan, arrives at the MC2, the last thing she's looking for is love. Her co-workers are surprised when Coal turns out to be female. Coal, used to the reaction, quickly earns the respect of the crew with her work ethic and skill with horses. Coal uses the strenuous work and friendship of the ranch hands to try and forget her broken past. Melissa Conway, owner of MC2, offers Coal a place to live in her home. They both are shocked to find they are linked in a way neither of them imagined. Mary Leah, Melissa's sister, arrives at the ranch to recover from a recent tragedy. The attraction between Mary Leah and Coal is instant and mutual. Can the three women survive their personal dilemmas? The love and friendship they develop certainly helps but will it be enough to bring them together. Ride along with the MC2, for boot scootin', butt kickin', dirt eatin', rodeo adventures, with a love story thrown into the mix.

If I Were a Boy—Erin O'Reilly Katie McGuire appears to have it all. A devoted husband, a job she loved, and a comfortable lifestyle. Helen Swenson is a successful financial director of a prominent investment firm, with an unfaithful husband, and few friends. Their husbands' annual trip to Padre Island National Seashore to reunite with their air force pilot squad becomes a pivotal point for the two women. Their lives take on a completely new meaning when an undeniable magnetism between them draws them together. Passion and secrecy becomes the norm, as they have no choice but to succumb to their attraction. Can the vacation love affair continue? When they leave for their respective homes, will they regret what happened? Life is not that easy to change and the people around them are the hardest to convince. There is no more powerful motivation than love. Except hate and there are plenty of people who want to see their relationship destroyed. Will Katie and Helen be able to make a life together work or succumb to doubts and the pressures of family? This story will fill you with the thrill of passion and the tenderness of love.

The Chronicles of Ratha: Book 1 Children of the Noorthi—Erica Lawson Jordana Laren is a hard-drinking, hard-fighting womanizer, who works as a freighter pilot in her spare time. Her latest customer drugs her, steals her ship, and abandons her on a desert hellhole called Rigeus, infamous penal planet for the worst women criminals. Her chances of survival aren't looking good. She has no food, water, or weapons, and the nearest bar is a million miles away. Just when she's ready to write her last will and testament, Jordana is rescued by a group of barely-clad women. Has she found nirvana? Her own personal harem seems like a possibility, until the intercession of their enemy, the Velkren. Their leader, Vel, remembers Jordana well, and not fondly. But why is Vel on this planet, surrounded by murderers, thieves, and bad-tempered bitches? Jordana knows Vel isn't a prisoner, so why is her nemesis on Rigeus mining mud, of all things? Jordana knows only one thing. She has to get off the planet before Vel kills her. Unfortunately, the women who saved her reveal themselves to be holy. They are the Noorthi, and Jordana's dream of endless debauchery becomes a nightmare of eternal servitude. The Noorthi make her one of them, marking her with a wrist tattoo, and leaving her no choice but to protect them with her life. The last thing Jordana wants is to become involved in galactic politics or heroic actions. But the tattoo ochre in her body is suddenly giving her morals and scruples, not to mention a better vocabulary! And she really can't pass up a chance to outwit Vel, whose megalomaniac plans are endangering not only the Noorthi, but the civilized galaxy itself. But Jordana is torn. Does she stop Vel at all costs, or does she get out from under the thumb of the Noorthi while she can? Some things were never meant to be easy...

Nesting—Renee MacKenzie Macy Stokes, a divorced mother who is struggling with her sexual identity, jumps at a once-in-a-lifetime opportunity to help her friends. She doesn't foresee it will put her in jeopardy of losing her son, Jeremiah. Fresh out of high school, Cam Webber travels to Augusta, Georgia, to reconcile with her aunt. When she learns that's impossible, she determines to gain acceptance from her aunt's partner, Sharon. Meanwhile, Cam sets her sights on Macy, but Macy has other ideas. Kenny Brewer is a good old boy who loves his wife, Dorianne, even when he thinks she's gone totally off her rocker. Dorianne gets it in her head that a local woman is her long-lost half-sister. But soon, her obsession with that is eclipsed by medical problems that involve them all. Set in Augusta, Georgia, *Nesting* explores the age-old issues of guilt, regret, and redemption, and the part they play in driving people to create and protect family-at any cost.

Reece's Faith—TJ Vertigo In the return of the main characters from the bestselling novel ***Private Dancer***, we see the blossoming relationship of bar owner, Reece Corbett and actress, Faith Ashford. The two women explore new, uncertain territory together, using sexual intimacy as a glue of comfort, helping them become strong and whole. A trusting Reece shares with Faith the sordid tale of how she became ***The Animal*** and Faith finds herself newly empowered by Reece's ongoing trust and support. Jealousy arises when Faith has to kiss a man on her TV show and two amorous women stalk Reece. When Faith is outed on her television show, things get crazy. With the arrival of her parents on the scene, the craziness escalates. As Faith tries to justify her lifestyle and defend her love for Reece, she discovers that nothing about her parents is as she once believed. This, not to be missed passionate and erotic romance, will have you begging for more.

Starting Over—Jen Silver Ellie Winters, a successful potter, is living on a remote hilltop farm inherited from her parents. Her well-ordered life is shaken apart when her past meets her present. Robin Fanshawe, Ellie's philandering long-term lover, has a fragile truce with Ellie. The arrival of women from Robin's present threatens to break that tentative pact. Charming Dr. Kathryn Moss, an archaeologist and an old lover of Ellie's, arrives on the farm searching for a new site to dig. When she discovers a previously unknown Roman settlement and ancient burial site on Ellie's farm, Ellie allows her to start an archaeological dig of the area. Will Ellie also allow the rekindling of an old romance or will she stay with Robin? Can that long term relationship, albeit tentative, recover from this collision or will an old romance trump everything she knows? Will Robin, seeing the interaction between Ellie and Kathryn, leave her womanising ways behind? Will she take a chance on giving herself wholly to the woman she loves? These questions and the mystery of whose royal resting place is disturbed at Starling Hill are answered in this classic romance of simmering passions, anguished loss, and the wonder of love.

E-Books, Print, Free e-books

Visit our website for more publications available online.

www.affinityebooks.com

Published by Affinity E-Book Press NZ LTD
Canterbury, New Zealand

Registered Company 2517228

www.ingramcontent.com/pod-product-compliance
Lightning Source LLC
Chambersburg PA
CBHW060551260626
47161CB00003B/1149